Pareidolia

A Novel
by
Paul Fronda

Pareidolia

First published in the United Kingdom in 2017
by Paul Fronda

This book is a work of fiction. Characters, names,
places, and incidents are of the author's
imagination and have been used fictitiously.
Resemblance to any events is entirely
coincidental.

Paul Fronda has asserted his moral right
to be identified as the author of this work.

Scripture quotations taken from the Holy Bible,
New International Version.
Copyright©1973,1978,1984 by International Bible
Society.
Used by permission.

Cover design by Martin Smith

Edited by Sheila Fronda

Proofread by Sheila Fronda

Copyright © Paul Fronda 2017

ISBN :9781544122762

Greater love has no one than this,
that he lay down his life for his friend.

Chapter One

"Chrissie! That son of yours is talking to himself again," Alan said, irritated at being woken from his sleep.

"Mmm?" she said, stirring.

"Your son. He's woken me up again! Look, I need to get some sleep. You know I've got to get up at four. For heaven's sake, go and shut him up for me, will you?"

"I'm sorry, Alan," she said, getting out of bed and going into her son's room. "Tommy, you have to be quiet. You're keeping Alan awake. You know he has to get up early, and he's getting cross."

"Sorry, Mummy. It's not my fault - it's my funny face stone. He keeps talking to me; I told him he will get me into trouble, talking."

"Look, Tommy, just go to sleep," she said, tucking him in.

"Who was he talking to this time?" Alan asked, not able to sleep until she came back.

"His stone."

"You need to take him somewhere. It's not natural for him to talk to a stone night after night. Sort it out tomorrow, will you?" he said, turning over.

She had met Alan, who was now her partner, two years ago when her husband left, and she knew that if he told her to do something he would expect it to be done, or she would suffer the consequences.

"I'd like to make an appointment for my son to see a doctor today," Chrissie said over the phone.

"Is it an emergency?" the receptionist asked.

Knowing that, if she hadn't done anything about Tommy when Alan came home he would be cross, she answered, "Yes!"

"This afternoon at 3 o'clock with Dr Williston," came a curt reply.

"Mrs Harvey, please sit down," Doctor Williston said. "Now what can I do for you?"

"It's Tommy, my son. He's having problems sleeping."

"Well, Tommy, what's keeping you awake then?" the doctor said, looking down at him.

"Funny face people," Tommy said, looking around at the room.

His mother sighed. "He talks to a stone, Doctor."

"Tommy, what do mean by 'funny face people'?" he asked.

Tommy, who was now more interested in climbing on the couch, didn't answer.

"Tommy! Come here and answer the doctor," his mother said, making him come and sit on her lap.

Tommy just sat there and looked at the doctor.

"Now Tommy, explain to me who the 'funny face people' are."

"They're in my room; some of them make me laugh, others scare me, but I have a special one. He's my friend; he talks to me."

"Okay, Tommy. Can you tell me where abouts in your room they live?" he asked.

"Everywhere," he said, jumping off his mothers lap.

"Tommy, come back here; the doctor has asked you a question!" she said, getting agitated with him. "Sorry, Doctor, he's not usually like this."

"Don't worry, Mrs Harvey. Tommy, tell me about the special stone that's your friend; tell me all about him."

Although Tommy was still exploring, the doctor's mention of 'friend' got his attention.

"I like him; he says that I'm his only friend and he likes talking to me, but when I leave my room he's lonely."

"So how old is your friend, Tommy?" the doctor asked.

"I don't know."

"Well is he big, small?"

"I don't know, but I can hold him in my hand."

"Okay, Tommy, now try and tell me, where do you see his face?"

"On the stone, but there's lots on my beach."

"You have a beach in your room?" the doctor said, humouring him.

"Not a real beach; the beach on my curtains!" Tommy replied, giggling.

Chrissie explained: "His father took him to the seaside where Tommy found a stone with a face on it and brought it home. Because he liked the beach so much, his father decorated his room with a seaside scene."

"I see, so you have the seaside in your room. That must be exciting," the doctor said.

"I have a pirate ship as well!"

"So, Tommy, is your special stone the one that came from the beach?"

"Yes, he's my special one with a funny face on; there's lots of them in the curtains but I don't think they like me because they don't talk to me. But he does. He's my friend."

The doctor finished writing his notes. "Well, Mrs Harvey, I don't think you've anything to worry about. I think he has an over-active imagination. Look, I'm going to prescribe a very light sedative to help him sleep. It should break the cycle."

"Thank you, Doctor," she responded, rising from her seat.

"Bye, Tommy," the doctor said.

"Bye . . ." he replied.

As Tommy and his mother approached the door, the doctor said, "Incidentally, Mrs Harvey, when did it start?"

"About two years ago. He was out with his father when he saw him disappear. Why? Do you think there's a connection?" she said, turning from the door.

"Can you explain what you mean — 'disappear'?"

"It's a long story doctor; let's just say he left?"

"Was he close to his father?"

"He was Daddy's boy; they were very close," she replied.

"Sometimes, when a child loses someone very close to them, they create a replacement," he said.

"Like an invisible friend?" she asked.

"You could call it that - hence Tommy talking to himself. Just give him the tablet before he goes to bed. Give it a few weeks and if he hasn't settled down, come back and see me."

"Thank you again, Doctor."

"Tommy, come and get your breakfast!" Chrissie called up the stairs.

There was no reply and she was concerned as he would usually have been scampering down into the kitchen at the mention of breakfast. The thought entered her head that maybe the sedative she had given him last night was the reason and that she had better check on him.

As she approached his door she could hear him talking and giggling. Listening outside, she thought she could hear another voice coming from the room.

Turning the door handle she quickly went in, to see Tommy standing in front of the curtains with a stone in his hand. Casually looking around the room, she asked, "Didn't you hear me, Tommy? I've been calling you for breakfast."

"Yes, I heard you, Mummy. I told Edward I have to go, but he didn't want me to. Sorry Mummy."

"Who is Edward, Tommy?" she asked, looking at the stones on the floor in front of the curtains.

"This one; hasn't he got a funny face?" he said, showing her the stone in his hand.

"How do you know his name is Edward?" she asked him.

"He's just told me."

As hard as she looked, Chrissie couldn't see anything resembling a face on the stone. Humouring Tommy, she said, "Hello Edward. Now you'd better get downstairs - there's a funny face on your egg."

"I won't be long, Edward, I promise," Tommy said.

"You've drawn a funny face on my egg," Tommy said, letting out a giggle.

"Yes, his name is Mr Boily."

"How do you know that?"

"Because he told me," Chrissie said, to see his reaction.

"Don't be silly, Mummy. Eggs can't talk."

"Nor can stones, Tommy," she said with a serious tone.

Having finished his breakfast, he said, "Can I go back and play with Edward now?"

Convinced that Edward was his invisible friend, she said, "Wash, and brush your teeth first and then you can play."

"He's at it again! I thought those pills were supposed to make him sleep!"

"I thought so too," she replied.

"Well they're not! Take him back to the doctor, will you. I've got to have my sleep."

"I'm sorry, Alan."

Chrissie went into Tommy's room, to find him sitting on the floor in front of the curtains again. "Now, that's enough, Tommy, get back into bed!"

Seeing that she was cross, Tommy said, "It's Edward, Mummy, he woke me up wanting me to talk to him."

Tucking him in, Chrissie said, "Now go to sleep." As she turned to go out of the door, she looked over at the stones.

"I mean it, Chrissie; I want you to do something about that boy!"

"Yes, Alan, I will."

In desperation on the phone, Chrissie managed to get an emergency appointment with the doctor that morning.

"So how's it been with him, Mrs Harvey?"

"I'm afraid the sedative didn't help; he's still talking to his invisible friend, Doctor."

"Would you say more, or less?"

"More! Now he says he calls his friend 'Edward'. It's every night and morning. It's causing problems with my partner not getting any sleep. And another thing, the other morning when I had to go and get him to come down for breakfast, I could hear another voice in the room. I'm worried; do you think he's developing schizophrenia?"

"No, Mrs Harvey, although schizophrenia can come about from a trauma, I don't think that's the case with Tommy. I think he's just playing, changing his voice. Most children do it when playing."

"Yes I understand that, but this wasn't Tommy's voice."

"I would think there's nothing to worry about, but to give you peace of mind, I'll write to a friend of mine, Doctor Freeman, who's a children's psychiatrist. I'm sure she will help this little fellow to sleep at night."

"I hope it won't take long. My partner is getting impatient with him, Doctor."

"I shouldn't think it would, Mrs Harvey, I'll tell her it's urgent."

"Thank you, Doctor Williston.

"Mrs Harvey, and you must be Tommy that I've heard so much about. Please take a seat," said Doctor Freeman.

"Thank you," she replied, sitting down.

"So, Mrs Harvey, I hear Tommy has had trouble sleeping? Can you tell me when it started?"

"About two years ago, when his father disappeared."

"Can you elaborate on 'disappeared'?"

"It was Tommy's birthday. We had arranged to take him to the seaside for the day, but I became ill and, so as not to disappoint him, Gordon, his father, took him. It was while they were on the way it happened.

A passing car stopped when they saw Tommy standing on his own by the side of the road, crying. When they asked where his mummy or daddy was, all they could get out of him was, "The face on the tree ate Daddy." They searched the nearby woods but didn't find any trace of him.

When the police brought Tommy home we managed to get out of him that his father had stopped at the roadside because Tommy wanted to go to the toilet and that when he had finished, he said to his daddy that he could see a face on a tree looking at him. Apparently Gordon went closer to the tree to see it. It was then that the tree, according to Tommy, ate him. The officer asked him what he meant by 'ate him' and he said that his daddy melted into the tree."

"And you say that was two years ago and he hasn't been seen since?" Doctor Freeman asked.

"That's right. I know what the police were thinking - that he left us, but the fact is that Gordon would never have left him alone in a wood. He adored Tommy. I'm sure something sinister has happened to him."

"Okay, that has helped me to get an idea of what's going on with Tommy.

Chapter Two

"Gordon found himself in a strange, dark void. Although he could sense something close to him he could not see it.

"Hello! Is there somebody there?" his voice echoed through the darkness.

There was no reply, only a feeling of a strange vibration that seemed to be scanning his mind.

"Can anyone tell me where I am?" he called out.

There was only silence.

"Anyone! Please! Someone speak to me!"

"It's a weird place, isn't it?"

"What was that? Who said that?"

"I said: it's a weird place."

Gordon looked around him, but all he could see was darkness, so thick that it could be cut by a knife. "Where are you?" he called out.

"Here!" a voice echoed from out of the darkness.

Gordon turned to where he thought the voice had come from.

"Where's 'here'?" Tom called out.

"Here," the voice said again.

Gordon once again turned, but still couldn't figure out where the voice was coming from, as it seemed to be coming from all directions at once.

"It's no good trying to figure out anything here, or trying to see. There's only an endless darkness where nothing makes sense," said the voice.

"So where am I? What is this place?" Gordon asked.

"It's nowhere; it's a place of nothingness," the voice replied.

"Have I died and gone to hell? But it can't be. Isn't hell supposed to be a place of fire? Maybe I have and this is a form of hell. What am I thinking? I don't believe in hell. Am I dead?" he said.

"Yeah you're dead; now shut up," another voice echoed from the darkness.

"Yeah, shut up; it ain't going to be long before the screaming starts and we don't need your whinging here," came yet another voice.

"Don't mind them; they've been here for ever. What was the last thing you remember?" the first voice asked.

Gordon thought. "I was . . . yes, I was with Tommy, looking at a face on a tree; then everything went weird and the next thing I know, I'm here."

"Who or what is a Tommy?" The voice asked.

"Tommy, is my . . . what was the question?" Gordon asked, feeling confused.

"Keep hold of what memories you have; the darkness here will soon consume them, then there's nothing."

"You talk as though this darkness is a living thing. It doesn't make sense to me - any of it. Am I dreaming?" Gordon said, now totally confused.

"No, it's no dream; the only real thing about this place is that it's real," the voice said.

"I can't see you, or work out where you are, but do you have a name?" Gordon asked.

"Name? I have forgotten what that is," the voice replied.

"You must have a name!" Gordon exclaimed.

"Must I? If I did have one, the darkness took it away."

"Well, how long have you been here?" Gordon asked.

There was silence; then the voice said, "I'm not sure. I just don't know."

"Are you saying that there's no time in this place?"

"As I said, there is nothing - just a dark void with no way out."

"There must be a way out of here! Has no one ever tried?"

"Why would you want to try when there is no way?" the voice said.

"Well, all I know is - I have to get back!" Gordon replied.

"Where's 'back'?" asked the voice.

"It's . . ." As hard has he tried, Gordon couldn't think where that was, but there was something inside him telling him that there was someone, or something, important waiting there for him.
"Well, I'm not staying here. I have hope in me. I'll find a way out if my names not . . ."

Gordon had a mental blank; his name was on the tip of his tongue.

"You can't remember the name can you? It's the darkness. The first thing it does is to remove your name from your mind and then all your memories."

"No! I won't let it take them. My name is Gor . . . This is crazy. Of course I know my name." He tried again. "Gor . . . Gordon!" He shouted out as it rolled off his tongue.

"Keep saying it. Where did that come from? Did I just say that? That's something new to me," the voice said.

"It's the start of hope," Gordon said.

"What's he on about: 'hope'? What's that? Whatever it is, it's no good here. Someone shut him up," a distant voice echoed.

"Yeah, he's upsetting the balance here," came another.

"What's up with these people here? Don't they like the word 'hope'?" Gordon said.

"They've been here so long, they're content in their ways. This 'hope' you speak of is new here."

"If all you people came here like me, you must have had hope?" Gordon said.

"Maybe we did, maybe we didn't, but we don't have it now (whatever hope is)," the voice replied.

"What's he talking about?" came a bewildered voice.

"Something about 'hope'," a voice answered.

"Hey you! If you have to talk, talk about something we understand will yah?" another voice called.

"Tell me what you understand and I'll talk about it!" Gordon called back.

There was silence.

"What, don't you want to talk now?" Gordon asked.

"That's the thing, we don't understand *anything* here," the voice near to him said.

Without warning, a scream that ripped through the darkness started a procession of screams that rang through Gordon's mind. He knew that wherever he was, it was a nightmare place of contagious despair and, if he was going to get back to his family (whatever that was), he was going to have to think fast while he still could, or end up like the rest of the mindless, tormented souls.

Chapter Three

"So tell me, Mrs Harvey, how are *you* coping? Are you sleeping?" Dr Freeman asked.

"I'm managing, but Alan isn't."

"And Alan is?"

"He's my partner," Chrissie replied, feeling guilty that it had only been two years and she was now living with another man.

Without passing any judgment, Dr Freeman knew that she would have to handle the situation carefully, as it was obvious that Tommy's traumatic experience (whatever had made his father disappear) was causing the problem and, to add to it, there was now another man that had come into his life, replacing his daddy.

"So, Tommy, I hear you have a funny face friend called Edward. Can you tell me about him?"

Tommy just sat on his mother's lap and didn't say anything.

"Tommy, tell the doctor about Edward," his mother said to him.

"I can't, Mummy."

"Why, Tommy?" she asked.

"It's a secret, Mummy. Edward said that I mustn't tell anyone about him anymore. If I do, he won't be my friend."

"That's all right, Tommy; we don't want that to happen do we?" said Doctor Freeman.

Tommy shook his head.

"Tommy, do you see Edward only in your room?"

"Yes, he lives at the seaside."

"It's a collection of stones he got from the beach," his mother said.

"Well, you're a lucky boy to have seaside stones in your bedroom," Doctor Freeman said.

"I've got pirates too!" Tommy said excitedly.

Doctor Freeman sat there and listened to Tommy telling her about the pirates. While he was chatting away, Doctor Freeman said to his mother, "Is he always as chatty as this?"

"He can be. I think it's the pirates that set him off. Tommy, that's enough now. The nice doctor here wants to talk to you."

Tommy went quiet.

"Tommy, apart from the stones in your bedroom, do you see funny faces anywhere else?"

"There's funny faces everywhere, but not all of them are funny. Some are scary and say nasty things to me," Tommy replied.

"They talk to you?" the doctor asked.

"Yes . . . I say hello to them; some say hello back, but some make scary noises. I like the fluffy clouds; there are some really, really big funny faces up there," Tommy replied.

"What about trees? Have you seen any funny faces in them?"

Tommy went quiet, then said, "Trees are scary; they eat you."

"Can you explain to me how they eat you?" the doctor asked.

"They open their mouth and gobble you up, like they did to Daddy in the woods. I don't like trees; they're nasty and scary."

"I think what Tommy is going through is traumatic stress. Can you tell me, Mrs Harvey, have you noticed him having any of these symptoms: becoming fearful, clingy and anxious when you leave him; irritable and disobedient;

21

bed-wetting, sucking his thumb, being preoccupied with thoughts and memories of the event?"

"I suppose most of them at first, then when he started talking to what he calls his funny faces, all those things stopped," she answered. So you say its 'traumatic stress'?" Chrissie said.

"Yes, what you have told me are the signs of traumatic stress.

Children can react in different ways to traumatic events. Their reaction may also depend on their age. All these are normal reactions to an extremely frightening event that he's been through.

But, with help and support from the people close to them, children begin to get over the shock in a few days, and usually recover after a few weeks. As for this talking to shapes that look like faces, I find it very interesting. Mrs Harvey, I'm going to suggest that we take Tommy back to the place where he experienced his trauma."

"Won't that set him back?" Chrissie asked.

"Having heard how scared Tommy is of trees, I feel if we can have him confront the actual tree and let him see that it's only a tree and it won't harm him, he will be on the road to recovery."

"Well, if you think it will help," Chrissie replied.

"Tommy, how brave are you?" Doctor Freeman asked.

"I'm very brave. I can fight monsters and dragons," he replied.

"Wow! You *are* brave. I have an adventure that needs a very brave young person to go on. As you're so brave, can I ask you to go on it with Mummy and I?" Doctor Freeman said.

"Are there monsters there?" he asked.

"There might be."

"Then I'll bring my sword," Tommy said. "When can we go?"

"Okay, Tommy, let me talk to Mummy. I'll check my schedule and let you know, hopefully later this week, Mrs Harvey, if that's okay with you?"

"Sooner the better, Dr Freeman."

"So how did it go today at the doctor's?" Alan asked.

"Yes – good; she thinks it will help if we take him back to the place where he saw his father disappear," Chrissie said.

"Won't that make him worse? The *last* thing I need is having less sleep!"

"That's what I thought, but she seems to think that, by taking him back to the root cause, it will be the start of his recovery," she replied.

"Well, I suppose if she thinks it will help, and there's a chance I might get my sleep, then go for it. How soon can she make this happen?"

"I'm waiting for her call; hopefully by the end of the week," Chrissie replied.

"Good! What's for tea?

Chapter Four

"**A**re you there?" Gordon called out.

"Yes, I'm here," the voice replied.

"Look, what about if I give you a name? That way, at least I know if it's you I'm talking to, and it will give you something to focus on," Gordon said.

"I don't know what 'focus' is. Anyway, even if I could do this 'focus' there would be no point; I won't remember it. The darkness will make sure of that."

"That's because you don't have anything to think about, but if you had a name and kept on saying it, you might just defeat the darkness. Surely you have to try, or are you too far gone as well?" Gordon said.

"I think I'd like to have a name," the voice replied.

"Then what's stopping you?"

"Nothing, I suppose. So what name would you give me?"

"Edward!" Gordon said.

"Why 'Edward'? Is that a good name?"

"I don't know why; it's the first name that came into my head and yes, I think Edward's a good name."

"Ed-wood, Edward! Yes I like it," the voice said. "And what do I call you?"

Gordon had to think. "Err . . . G, G, G, blast you, whatever you are. You will not take my name!"

He searched deep within his mind, and then it came to him, "Gordon!" he shouted.

There was a hissing sound, followed by a wave of vibration that rippled throughout the place and seemed to go on and on.

"What was that?" Gordon asked.

"It happens occasionally, when the balance here has been upset," Edward replied.

"Good, and there will be more! Do you hear me, whatever you are, there will be more!" Gordon shouted at the top of his voice.

There was an eerie silence. "Are you there, Edward?" Gordon called out.

There was no reply. "Edward, it's me, Gordon. Are you there?"

A deafening hissing sound started to fill the place and, before Gordon knew what was happening, he found that he was looking out into a mass of trees, but couldn't understand how. It was as if he was inside the tree looking out.

"You finished?" came a voice from somewhere near him.

"What? What do you mean finished?" Gordon answered.

"You can't stay here. There're others waiting to gather them in," said the voice.

Before Gordon knew it he was back in the darkness again.

"Edward, you there?" he called out.

"Are you talking to me or someone else now?"

"Yes you, Edward."

"Oh yes, that's my name isn't it?"

"That's right, it's Edward," Gordon replied. "What just happened?"

"You mean the hissing then the gathering?"

"What's gathering?" Gordon asked.

"It's what always happens. We all just find ourselves looking out into another place. Most of the time there's not darkness but something else. I have no name for it," Edward said.

Gordon pondered for a moment, then said, "I think it's called l . . ." The word had gone from his mind. "What's the opposite of dark?" he asked himself. "Think man." He could feel his mind straining for the word. "That's it . . . of course, it's light!"

"Light?" Edward said, intrigued with a new word.

"So why does it happen?" Tom asked.

"So that we can gather," Edward said.

"Gather what?" Gordon said, not understanding.

"I'm not too sure, but when we do, there are others here to join us. One thing I do know, it's our sole purpose."

"But how?" Gordon asked.

"I don't know how; all I know is that when we go out to the other place sometimes there's others that come back with us," Edward replied.

"Like me?"

"I suppose so," Edward said.

"Then who was it that brought me here? Was it you?" Gordon asked.

"I think you said you were looking at a tree, didn't you? Or did I imagine that?"

"Yes, a tree. That's where I was just then, after the hissing came. I think it was the same tree that I was looking at before I was brought here. I don't know how, but something deep inside me tells me so," Gordon replied.

"Then it wasn't me, I'm assigned to a . . . ? No, it's gone. I don't know what it is," Edward sighed.

"So then, I seem to have got here by a tree, and you don't remember how you got here?"

Edward tried to think, "My mind is blank, Gordon."

"Concentrate, Edward," Gordon said.

"I'm trying, but I can feel the darkness trying to stop me."

Gordon had an idea that, if somehow he could distract the darkness away from Edward, he might have a chance of remembering.

"My name is Gordon! Do you hear? Gordon! And I'm getting out of here!" he shouted out.

Instantly a vibration wave went through Gordon. His cries of pain could be heard throughout the voids of darkness.

"I think I'm remembering. There's a rhythm of water washing over my feet and being hot, Gordon."

There was no reply.

"Gordon, are you there?" Edward called out.

There was only a murmur.

"Are you alright, Gordon? Speak to me."

"Edward, is that you?" came a weak reply.

"Yes it's me. I've remembered!"

"What was it that you remembered?" Gordon asked.

"You asked me if I remembered how I got here."

"Did I?"

"Yes, I remembered water and being hot."

Gordon's mind cleared enough to ask: "That's good; anything else?"

Edward thought again. "Whatever I was walking on was uncomfortable."

"Beach stones!" Gordon managed to say, feeling a little stronger.

"Beach . . . Yes! I was at the beach. I remembered!" Edward shouted.

A wave in the darkness shook the place again, aimed at Edward.

With little strength he whispered, hoping the darkness couldn't hear, "I remembered; I was fascinated by a face on a stone, so I picked it up and then, like you, something happened that brought me here."

"That's good, Edward."

"What - that I'm here?" Edward asked.

"No, that you remembered how you got here; you got here through a stone."

The place shook violently.

"Mummy, where are you? I want to go home," sobbed a child.

"It takes children as well! What is this evil thing?" Gordon said angrily.

"Is that a child? Then there are lots of them here, but their noise doesn't last for long. Is it because a child is small and hasn't got many memories?" Edward asked Gordon.

Gordon found it hard to answer as his capacity for thinking was now limited and he was trying to fathom how, by looking at the shape of a face, you could end up here.

"Edward, I think I partially understand what's happening here. It's the faces. It was the face on a tree that brought me here; the face on a stone that brought you, and I suppose it's the same for others here. But how can looking at the shape of a face do that?"

His mind hurt with the questions that were coming to it. Gordon spoke out loud. "Does it happen to everyone? Does it possess your soul? And leave the body behind?"

"What's a 'body'?" Edward asked.

"You must know what a body is; every one has one," Gordon replied.

"Sorry, Gordon, no," he answered.

Gordon couldn't see his body so, to reassure himself, he felt for it. There was nothing. He came to the conclusion that somehow all he consisted of was an entity of thoughts and memories in a weird world of darkness that was slowly erasing them.

He could feel himself being drawn away from what he was trying to figure out.

"No! I know what you're trying to do," he said aloud.

Gordon knew he had to concentrate.

"There's a name for this phenomenon - where some people see shapes of faces or other things in random patterns, but, for the love of me, I can't think what it is. And it's not you, darkness, that's keeping it from me. Do you hear me, darkness! It's not you this time keeping it from me?" he said.

Gordon felt another wave go through him, which told him the darkness had heard him.

"But this transporting from one place to another - I can't get my head around it. So, Edward, the hissing moment, do you know where you went to gather?" Gordon asked him.

Edward replied, "I'm not quite sure, but I think I should be gathering on the beach, but the place, it's not the beach. It's the place of the same small person every time."

"Why don't you gather him?" Gordon asked.

"At first I tried, but there was something about the small person stopping me," Edward replied.

"When you say: 'small person', it sounds like, either it's a midget, or a child," Gordon said.

"This is so good, Gordon! I can remember so much. You are right - I can remember things when I really try. I don't think it's a midget."

"Are you sure you can remember what a midget looks like?"

"I think so, Gordon; anyway I'm sure it's a child because it makes little noises."

Gordon tried to decipher what he meant by 'little noises'. "Do you mean talking?"

"No, I know talking; the noise is something that he does after - when I stop talking."

"What? Are you saying that you talk to him and he can hear you?"

"Yes, Gordon, and I can hear him."

"What do you talk about?" Gordon enquired.

"My name, and that I live in a stone. These things I couldn't answer as I didn't know, but, thanks to you, I can now."

"I think I've got it. The noise you mentioned. It could be 'giggling'."

"Yes! Of course, Gordon, it's giggling. How could I forget that?"

"I can see that, being here, it's easy. You know, Edward, it's just dawned on me that we can communicate with the outside, and you say hope is dead here. Far from it, Edward. Far from it!

Whatever you are out there: do you hear? There's hope here!" Gordon shouted.

The darkness unleashed a shock wave directed at Gordon that sent a pain through him, as though he had been slashed with a sharp knife.

"Ahhh . . . " came from Gordon. Everything went blank.

"Are you okay, Gordon? I lost you there for a while," Edward asked.

"I think so. What happened?"

"I think you did something the darkness didn't like, Gordon."

"The *what*?"

"Don't you remember, Gordon . . . the darkness."

"Who's Gordon?"

"You are. It's taking your memories, Gordon." In desperation, Edward applied the same tactics that Gordon had used to help him. "Say your name, Gordon, please! I don't want to go back to how things were," Edward pleaded.

"Gordon. I'm Gordon. My name is Gordon and you're Edward."

"Yes, I am. That's me (I think). G . . . Gor . .don, I'm losing it! It's starting to erase my mind!"

Gordon realised that, if he didn't do something, it would only be a moment before Edward's mind was gone. As weak as he was from the onslaught by the darkness, he managed to say, "Edward, repeat after me: 'My name is Edward'. Say it, man!" Gordon knew that, if he didn't, it would all be over for the pair of them.

"Edward, Edward, Edward . . ."

"That's it. Keep saying it. Gordon, Gordon, Gordon . . ." he chanted in unison.

"I'm glad you're back, Edward. I've been calling you. I take it you've been to the same place?" Gordon asked.

"Yes. I told him I now have a name; he said he liked it and asked if we could be friends. What's a friend?"

"A friend is . . . " The word seemed distant to him. "I'm sure it's where two people are close," Gordon said, struggling with the reply.

"Are we friends, Gordon?"

"I suppose, as we talk to each other we must be, I think."

"I don't think I've had a friend and now I've got two," Edward said, sounding pleased.

"Does the child have a name?"

"Is it Tommy?" he asked Gordon.

"I don't know, Edward; I wasn't there, although the name seems to have a meaning to me. Oh, I wish my mind wasn't so sketchy," Gordon sighed. "Edward, the next time you're there, will you tell him about me?"

"Will Tommy know you then?"

"I don't know. I don't even know why I asked. Should he? He's only a child."

"Can I tell him your name and that you're my friend?" Edward asked.

"Who?"

"Tommy - my friend, Gordon!"

"Oh yes, Tommy, sure."

"Have you gathered yet?" Edward asked.

"No. I've been to my tree but I've seen nobody, just other trees," Gordon replied.

"You will. There's no hurry here. What's that word you used - 'time'?

"Yes, you have all the time in the . . ."

"World, Edward, world," Gordon said.

"I think us talking to each other has helped us to retain our memories, don't you think, Gordon?"

"What was that Edward?"

Chapter Five

Doctor Freeman, with Tommy and his mother, pulled into the lay-by.

"Is this where the monsters live?" Tommy asked, holding his sword.

"Yes, Tommy. Are we ready to go and find them?" Doctor Freeman asked him.

"Yes," he replied, undoing his seatbelt and opening the door.

"Slow down, Tommy. Wait for us," his mother said.

As Tommy approached the woods, he stopped and turned.

"What's wrong, Tommy? Why did you stop?" Doctor Freeman asked.

"Trees!" he said.

"They're only trees Tommy - they can't hurt you," she replied.

His mother could see how scared he was. "It's all right, Tommy -I'm here. We will go into the woods together," she said, taking his hand.

Tommy gained confidence as he went into the trees, eventually letting go of his mother's hand.

"This way, Tommy!" his mother called out to him as he ran off, a distance in front of them.

"You know where the tree is, Mrs Harvey?"

"It's been two years, but I remember; it's only a little way from the road. I'm sure it's over here," she said, leading the way. "That's the tree, the big one over there."

"Tommy, this is where the monster lives; do you think you can find it?"

Tommy looked all around him. "I can't see it, but I've got my sword ready."

"Let's stay here and see if Tommy recognises the tree," Doctor Freeman said.

Tommy slashed at the bushes with his sword, shouting, "I'll find you, monster! Take that!"

"He seems to be taking no notice of the trees," his mother said.

"That's what I was hoping," the doctor replied.

Suddenly, Tommy stopped playing. He was standing still, facing the big tree.

"What's wrong, Tommy?" the doctor asked.

"This tree is a bad tree. It took Daddy. Give me back my daddy! Give me back my daddy!" Tommy shouted, slashing at the tree with his sword.

Tommy's mother was about to go to him, when Doctor Freeman stopped her.

"Leave him - it's a part of him opening up," she said.

Gordon's conversation with Edward was stopped short by the hissing. Instantly he found himself back at the tree. But this time it was different. He could see a child in front of him shouting. Looking down at the child, Gordon could feel something stirring deep in his mind, but couldn't grasp what.

It was the words he heard. "That's it, Tommy; let it all out." There was something important about the name 'Tommy'.

"Tommy!" he found himself saying.

When Tommy heard his daddy's voice coming from the tree, saying his name, he stopped slashing at it and said, "Daddy?"

The word 'Daddy' started to clear the fog in his mind, revealing a kaleidoscope of images of him, the child and a woman.

"Tommy! It's me – Daddy!" he called out to him.

"Daddy! Daddy, I've missed you. When are you coming home?"

"Is he talking to his daddy?" Doctor Freeman said to his mother.

"It sounds like it. I think being at the spot where his daddy disappeared is doing it all right. He hasn't said the word 'daddy' since the police brought him home (apart from in your surgery)," she replied.

"Leave him for a while longer. I'd like to see what he does next," the doctor said.

"Tommy, I'm trapped here! I'm trying to find my way out. Tell Mummy."

"Mummy! Daddy's trapped inside the tree; he can't get out. We have to help him!" Tommy cried out.

"Hey, you! Are you going to gather this one or not? Because I'll have him. Children are good to gather - they are soon quiet," came a voice close to Gordon.

Gordon could feel something starting to pull him away from the tree.

"Run, Tommy; get out of here!" Gordon shouted at him.

"No, Daddy - I want you to come home with me!"

"Go! Go now!" Gordon shouted again.

Tommy just stood there, not understanding why his daddy should say that.

Gordon tried with all his strength to resist the pull, but could feel himself getting weaker. He knew if Tommy stayed there, he would be gathered by the evil within. So, as much as he didn't want to, he knew he would have to say something that would make Tommy go from the place.

"I don't want to come home. Now get out of here and don't come back!" he shouted.

Tommy ran to his mother crying, "Daddy shouted at me! He doesn't want to come home."

His mother cuddled him. "Doctor Freeman, I think it's time to leave!" she said, concerned.

On their way home, Tommy asked, "Mummy, why didn't Daddy want to come home?"

"I don't know why, Tommy," she answered, holding back tears at seeing him so hurt.

Pulling up outside their home, Doctor Freeman said, "I was hoping it would have gone better than that. He was doing well until that tree. There's something deep there; I'm afraid it's going to take more time than I thought. Can you bring him to me next week?"

"Yes . . ." his mother replied, worried about what she would tell Alan when he asked.

Chapter Six

Gordon found himself back in the darkness. Whatever had just happened to him had left a feeling in him that he couldn't understand. There such emptiness and despair that he wanted to talk to someone, but he couldn't think who.

"Gordon, are you there?" came a voice.

"Is someone saying something?" Gordon answered.

"It's me, Edward, remember?"

The name Edward rekindled a memory. "I think so . . ."

"Where am I?" Gordon replied.

"It's the darkness, Gordon. Fight it! Say your name," Edward encouraged.

"I'm Gordon; my name is Gordon. Yes, the darkness; this place - it's coming back. I've just come back from the tree. Oh, why does it hurt so much?" he shouted.

"What's that word, Gordon – 'hurt'?" Edward asked.

"I don't know; it's something that's going through me. It's like a memory that's being torn away from me, that I think was important to me. It was something at the tree."

"Oh, that's what it is. I get that every time I come back from visiting Tommy, my friend. Now I know it's called 'hurt'," Edward replied.

"That's it! It's something to do with that name that's causing the hurt," Gordon said.

"Now you told me about hurt (and it's not a nice word) I am getting to understand that every time we are sent to gather, it's also to cause us to hurt," Edward concluded.

"There's nothing nice about this place. It's a place of torment and pain. *Why am I here? What did I do wrong?*" Gordon shouted into the darkness.

"Shut up or we will all suffer!" shouted a voice.

Calming down, Gordon asked, "Did you see your small friend, Edward?"

"No, he wasn't there. Sometimes the other being takes him away, but only for what seems a short while. This time he didn't come back and then the pull brought me back here. Maybe I will next time," Edward said, sounding disappointed.

"Edward, you know how we try to help each other not to forget? When you ask me something, make sure I answer you quickly, because if I have to think about it, the words go."

"Yes, Gordon, I've noticed. I think that, since you have been here, the darkness doesn't like it and is directing its force at you."

"And you, I think," Gordon said.

"I don't think I'm so much of a threat. It knows me and can erase my memory whenever it likes, but you seem to be a problem for it. You know that word you taught me - 'light"? Well, you're like that in this place; it's different since you've been here," Edward said.

"How long have I been here then?" he asked.

"I'm not sure, Gordon."

Chrissie and Tommy arrived home.

"So, how did it go with him this time?" Alan asked.

"Tommy, you can go to your room and play. I'll be up later to see you," she said, not wanting him to hear the conversation that was about to take place.

"So?" Alan said, waiting.

"Yes – good. The doctor seems to think there was a break- through and he will get better soon," she lied.

"Good, because if not, I was going to suggest that he goes to live with his granny. Now, how long before I get something to eat?"

Not wanting to upset him, Chrissie got on with his meal.

"Are you okay, Tommy?" Chrissie said, going into his room with a glass of warm milk.

"I don't like Alan, Mummy. He's always cross with you. I wish Daddy was home."

"I know, Tommy, so do I," she said, giving him a cuddle. "Listen, no talking tonight. Now, drink your milk and sleep. Night, night," she said, kissing him on the forehead.

"Goodnight, Mummy."

"Well, I'm going to bed; I've got an early start. Don't wake me up coming to bed, do you hear!" Alan said to her.

The worry of telling Alan about Tommy brought on a headache, so she took a strong pill. She sat in her chair, listening out in case Tommy started talking, but the effects of the pill were making her eyes heavy. She knew she had to get to bed before sleep overcame her.

She was abruptly woken by the words, "That's it, I've had enough! I'm going to do what his father should have done!" Alan ranted, getting out of bed and heading for Tommy's room.

"Don't you hurt him!" Chrissie cried out, rushing after him.

The noise of the door suddenly bursting open made Tommy look up.

"Give me that!" Alan shouted, as he snatched the stone out of his little hand.

With the stone in one hand he raised his other to hit Tommy, but was stopped by Chrissie holding on to it and screaming, "No, don't hurt him!"

Alan turned and, with the powerful arm that Chrissie had hold of, he threw her to the floor.

"Mummy, Mummy!" Tommy cried, trying to get to her, but was stopped by Alan who had now raised his hand to him again.

"What the . . .?" Alan said, turning to look at his arm that was holding the stone. It was dissolving into the stone!

His screams filled the room, while Chrissie looked on in disbelief as his entire body disappeared into the stone. The silence in the room was broken by, "Mummy, are you okay?"

Chrissie took her eyes off of the stone, which was now lying on the floor, and went to Tommy.

"Yes, I'm okay. Did he hurt you?"

"No, Mummy. Edward stopped him - he's my friend."

Chrissie didn't know what to say. She quickly held his hand and took him to her bed. Still not believing what she had just witnessed, she lay there cuddling Tommy until she fell asleep.

The phone ringing woke her up. She looked at the bedside clock and could see that it was past nine. Seeing Tommy, fast asleep next to her, made her think that what she had seen might not have been a dream. Tommy would *never* have been allowed in her bed if Alan was around.

Quickly she went downstairs to answer the phone.

"Mrs Harvey, it's Dr Freeman. Are you and Tommy available Friday this week?"

Chrissie didn't answer as she had to think. Eventually she managed to say, "Dr Freeman, sorry. What was that?"

"I asked if Friday was okay for you and Tommy to come and see me?"

"Err . . . Friday, you say? I think so."

"Are you okay, Mrs Harvey? You sound as though something's wrong."

"Wrong . . . Er, no – nothing's wrong, I . . . everything is all right," she stammered

"Are you sure? You don't sound as if it is."

There was a pause. "No, it's not all right, Dr Freeman. I don't know what's happening to me. Last night I witnessed something that's impossible."

Chrissie spilled out what she had seen.

"And you say Tommy saw it as well?" Doctor Freeman asked.

"Yes, I was more shocked than him. He said something about Edward protected him," Chrissie responded.

"How's Tommy now? Has he said anything about it?"

"No, he's still asleep in my bed; I had to get him out of that room."

Dr Harvey's suspicions about Chrissie were now aroused. Maybe the problem was with the *mother*, and that was affecting Tommy.

"Look, Mrs. Harvey, having heard what you've told me, I think I should come on over. I feel there's something going on with Tommy that's not right. Will that be okay?"

"Well yes . . . I think I agree with you, Dr Freeman," Chrissie said, relieved that she would have someone to talk to.

The silence of the darkness was once more disturbed. It was the voice of Alan.

"Where am I? What is this place? Is there anybody
there . .? Someone, please help me . . ."

Alan's words disappeared into the darkness.

"You there, Gordon?"

A voice that sounded vacant answered, "I think I know who's asking. Ed . . .ward?"

"Yes, Gordon, it's me. Can I talk to you?"

"Yes, I have no one else to talk to," Gordon replied.

"I have just had something new happen. I have questions for you. I was at the place of my friend, Tommy, and we were talking when a different person came into the place. His voice was loud - directed at Tommy. I sensed a strange look in Tommy's eyes as he looked at the person. Whatever it was that put it there made me . . . ; I can't describe the word I'm looking for, but I gathered the person. Then the feeling changed; it made me feel different. They're my questions, Gordon; what were those feelings? Oh, you said to remind you to not think about the questions when I asked."

"Did I . . .?"

"Gordon! Don't think, just tell me the answers," Edward said.

"Feelings . . . you say it was when you saw something in Tommy's eyes. I would say you saw fear in his eyes and you reacted by gathering the man."

"Yes! It made me want to do it," Edward said.

"Could it be 'anger' that came upon you?"

"What about the last one, it was so different?" Edward asked.

"Err . . . Tell me again, I'm having trouble trying to think," Gordon pleaded.

"It was the feeling after I gathered him," Edward replied.

"Gathered . . . yes! It could be 'satisfaction' or 'pleasure' maybe; either of those would make sense. But then does anything make sense here?" Gordon said, his mind slipping back into blankness.

Edward could be heard in the darkness, repeatedly saying his newfound words.

Chapter Seven

Hearing the doorbell, Chrissie made her way to the door. It was Doctor Freeman.

"I'm so glad you came over. I don't know what I've have done, after seeing what I did," Chrissie said, showing her in.

As they sat down at the table, Doctor Freeman said, "Now, tell me again exactly what happened."

Chrissie told her from the beginning what had taken place.

"Where's Tommy now?" the doctor asked.

"He's upstairs in my room. He wanted to go into his own room, but I wouldn't let him," Chrissie replied.

"I would like to see him; can you call him down?"

"Tommy!" Chrissie called up the stairs, "The nice doctor is here to see you! Can you come down now please?"

Tommy came scampering down the stairs.

"Hello, Tommy. What have you been up to?" the doctor asked.

"I've been talking to the faces in Mummy's room."

"Where? What faces, Tommy?" his mother asked, alarmed that there were more faces that Tommy could see.

"On your pretty curtains, Mummy; there's lot of them."

"Tommy, you say you've been talking to *them*; do they talk back?" the doctor asked.

"No . . . they're not like Edward. He's nice - he always talks to me," Tommy replied.

"Tommy, can you show me the faces in Mummy's room? (If that's alright with you, Mrs Harvey?)" the doctor asked.

"Yes, of course. Tommy, show the nice doctor."

Tommy excitedly raced up the stairs to the room.

"So where are they, Tommy?" The doctor asked.

Standing in front of the curtains, Tommy said, "There's one down here, one over there, one up there and one here, oh - and one hiding here."

54

Both the doctor and his mother studied closely, but couldn't see any faces. All they could see were the patterns in the material.

"Tommy, I can't see any faces; do you think you can very slowly point out the eyes, nose and mouth of one of the faces for me?"

Tommy look surprised that the doctor couldn't see them.

"Eyes, nose, and mouth!" he said, pointing.

Once Tommy had pointed the features out, she could make out that the swirls of the pattern could resemble a face.

"Okay, Tommy, can you show me Edward?" the doctor asked him.

"He doesn't live in Mummy's room; he's in my room, but Mummy won't let me see him," he said, dejectedly.

"Mrs Harvey, I think it's important that I see his room and this stone," she said, turning to her.

"It's the room opposite," Chrissie said, nodding despondently.

Hearing that, Tommy rushed off ahead towards his room.

"Tommy wait!" his mother called out, fearful of what might be in there.

But it was too late. Tommy went rushing in to pick up the stone from where it had fallen on the floor.

"Here is Edward!" he said, showing the doctor.

Dr Freeman could see a white stone with some dark markings on it.

"So this is Edward?" the doctor asked.

"Yes."

"Can I hold it?" she asked.

"Oh, please be careful, Dr Freeman!" Chrissie implored, scared that she'd suffer the same fate as Alan.

"Tommy, do you think, if I held Edward, he would hurt me?"

"He won't if I tell him you're my friend. Edward this is my friend. I don't want you to hurt her," he said, talking to the stone.

The doctor and his mother waited. Having witnessed the event of Alan being drawn into the stone, Chrissie half-expected to hear a voice, but there was nothing.

Playing along with Tommy, the doctor asked, "What did he say Tommy?"

"He said that it's only me that can hold him, otherwise he couldn't stop you being gathered."

"Tommy, ask him what does he mean: 'gathered'?"

"Edward, my doctor friend wants to know what you mean by *gathered?*"

Tommy stood there looking at the stone as if waiting for the reply.

"He said it's what happened to the man that tried to hurt me."

"Ask him where the man is now?" the doctor prompted.

"He's been gathered to where Edward lives."

"And where's that, Tommy?"

"Inside the stone!" Tommy said, as if everyone knew.

"Okay, Tommy, can we go back downstairs now?" said the doctor. Tommy looked at his mother, who could see he didn't want to.

"Come on Tommy, leave Edward there," Chrissie said to him.

Putting the stone on his bedside table he said, "I've got to go now Edward, but I'll be back soon."

"Mrs Harvey, I would like to arrange for Tommy to have some tests with a specialist. I think whatever's going on with him is beyond my scope. So, if that's alright with you, I'll make arrangements?"

"But what about what I saw? Do I need to see someone?" Chrissie said, alarmed.

"As I said, Mrs Harvey, I'm sorry, but what's going on here is beyond me."

As the doctor made her way to the door, Chrissie implored:

"Do I report him missing?"

The doctor didn't answer. She was considering reporting Chrissie to the authorities concerned with child protection, but it might be better to wait until a specialist could assess her state of mind.

"Don't worry, Mummy. Edward and I will look after you now Alan has gone," Tommy said, taking her hand.

Chrissie couldn't stop the little tear that ran down her cheek.

She realised it would only be a matter of time before someone would be knocking at her door asking where Alan was. She knew that if she told the truth she wouldn't be believed. It might even be decided that she was losing her mind, and that Tommy should be taken away from her; or, worse, she could be suspected of murdering Alan. So she decided to say that he had walked out on her and she didn't know where he was. That would be a credible explanation, as it must happen all the time.

Tommy's appointments with the specialists dumbfounded them. With her new explanation about Alan's disappearance, Chrissie seemed to show no signs of mental illness and Dr. Freeman's concerns were shelved. All they could come up with was that hopefully he would grow out of it as he got older, but the memory of what happened to his father stayed deep within him.

"Wake up, Tommy. You don't want to be late on your first day of senior school! Hurry up and get ready, while I go and get your breakfast. And make sure you comb your hair," his mother said opening the curtains.

Tommy stirred, got himself ready and made his way downstairs.

"Now, I want you to do well today and that means being on your best behaviour. Do you hear?"

"Yes, Mum, I hear you," he replied.

"And don't forget your glasses, bus fare and lunch. You have a nice day at school and I'll see you when you get home," Chrissie said, kissing him goodbye.

Tommy was apprehensive about the first day as he didn't know anybody, but his mum's words, "You'll soon make friends," gave him comfort.

"Hey, Geek! What have you got for lunch there?" Frampton said.

"Peanut butter sandwich," Tommy answered reluctantly, realising that it was the school bully asking.

"I don't like that stuff, but it will have to do; hand it over!" Frampton demanded.

Frampton was head and shoulders taller, and Tommy handed it over.

The school day came to an end and Tommy couldn't wait to get home, as he was ravenously hungry. He was making his way to the bus stop, when a hand grabbed his shoulder from behind.

"Hey, Geek, how much money you got?" It was Frampton.

"Just my bus fare," Tommy replied.

"Well, you don't now. Hand it over!"

"No, I won't," Tommy said, nervously standing up to him.

The next thing Tommy knew was he was on the ground, after a punch from Frampton.

"But how am I supposed to get home?" Tommy cried out, as Frampton went through his pockets and took the money.

"Walk! Exercise is good for you," Frampton said, laughing has he walked away with his money.

"What happened to you, Tommy? You're so late! And what happened to your face?" his mother asked, alarmed.

Tommy didn't want his mother to know about what happened to him, as he knew she would make things worse by coming to the school.

"I fell over and it made me miss the bus, so I walked," he told her. "How long before tea's ready - I'm starved?"

"I'll pack a bit more in your lunchbox tomorrow. We can't have a growing lad going hungry can we? Food will be about half an hour. Why don't you go upstairs and clean yourself up? I'll call you when it's ready."

"Hello, Tommy. I'm pleased your home."

"I hate school, Edward!"

"That's not like you, Tommy; have you had a bad day?" Edward asked.

"Yes," Tommy went on to tell Edward what had happened.

"This boy doesn't sound like a nice person. Can I help you in any way?"

"How can you help me, Edward?"

"Why don't you take me to school tomorrow?"

A grin came on Tommy's face.

"What have you got for my lunch today, Geek?" Frampton asked cockily.

"If you promise to leave me alone, I'll show you something that no one else knows about, after school," Tommy said.

"So, what is this something?"

"I can't show you now, but if you come to the park alone after school, I'll show you."

"It had better be something good, Geek, or I'll bash your brains out this time," Frampton responded.

"I promise you it will be good - that's for sure," Tommy said, smiling.

"So where is it?" Frampton asked.

Looking around, Tommy could see that there were a few people walking their dogs. "Let's go over there behind the toilet block; I don't want anyone else to see it - only you."

"Okay. Now show me!" Frampton demanded.

Tommy took the stone from his pocket. "Here it is."

"What's special about that? It's just a stone. You got me all the way here to look at a *stone*. Now I'm going to bash your brains out!" he said angrily.

"Wait! It has a face on it," Tommy said, cowering.

"I can't see a face!" Frampton said.

"Well, if you take it and look closer you will."

Frampton snatched the stone out of Tommy's hand and examined it.

"Can you see it?" Tommy said pointing out the face, making sure Frampton didn't miss it.

Frampton stared at it, then said, "Yeah, I can see it!"

The minute he said that, Tommy said, "Now, Edward!"

Tommy walked out from behind the toilets and made his way home with a smug look on his face, knowing that he wouldn't be bothered by a bully again.

And so the years passed and Tommy grew. Through his conversations with Edward, he began to get an inkling of this strange other world and the evil contained in it. He began to understand why his father, who loved him so much, would shout at him and tell him to go away. Once he could drive he made many visits to the tree to talk to his father, and asked many questions about what was it like where he was. But, with every visit he made, his father was more vague about who his son was. As he had promised his father that he would find a way back for him, he read and studied every book on the paranormal he could lay his hands on, which led to him becoming a leading expert on the subject.

Chapter Eight

"Good day at the office, Alice?" Alec asked.

"Manic – as usual. And you?"

"A meeting about fundraising for the church building."

"So how's it going?"

"Slow, but I know if we keep praying we'll get there," Alec replied.

"I did manage to grab half an hour at lunch time. Funnily enough I was reading in the local paper that there's a talk on that stuff you were telling me about last Sunday," Alice said.

"What stuff?" he asked.

"You know, when that doctor chap came up to you after the service and said he thought he was possessed, because he kept seeing shapes that resembled faces and hearing voices. You did tell me what they call it. What was it?" Alice asked.

"Pareidolia."

"That's it. Anyway, there's a professor at the University talking about it tonight. Do you fancy going?"

"I must confess when the doctor spoke to me about what he was seeing and hearing, I did feel it was something I knew next to nothing about. Maybe, by going, I'd be more help to him. Did it say what time?" he asked.

"7.30."

"Do you think we'll have time to get some food and change?"

"Well, if we stand here and talk about it, no. You go and change and I'll get us something quick to eat," Alice replied.

The room quickly started to fill. Alec and Alice sat near the front, as being there would make it easier to ask questions. The room went quiet as the speaker walked in.

"Good evening, my name is Tom Harvey. For the next hour I'll be talking on the subject of 'Pareidolia'. We will be discussing in depth what

Pareidolia is and why it only affects some people. At the end the floor will be open for Q & A.

Okay, let's start with the meaning of the word. It is derived from the Greek words: 'para' (meaning: something faulty, wrong, instead of), and the noun, 'eidōlon' (meaning: image, form or shape). Pareidolia is a psychological phenomenon involving a stimulus (an image or a sound) wherein the mind perceives a familiar pattern of something, where none actually exists. Most people have never heard of Pareidolia. But nearly everyone has experienced it.

The most common examples that are perceived are images of animals, faces, or objects in cloud formations, the man in the moon, and hidden messages within recorded music played in reverse or at higher- or lower-than-normal speeds.

People have long seen faces in the moon, in oddly-shaped vegetables and even burnt toast."

A ripple of laughter broke out in the room.

The professor's talk soon came to an end and Alec listened intently to the questions and the answers that were given, but no one asked the question he had. The meeting came to an end.

"Why didn't you ask him your question - about voices associated with it?" Alice asked.

"I thought I'd try and talk to him after."

Alec and Alice sat there waiting for the others to finish talking to the professor and thanking him for the talk. Eventually they were the only ones left in the room with Tom Harvey, who was clearing away his notes.

"That was a interesting talk," Alec said.

"Thank you. Yes, it is an interesting subject. Have you experienced Pareidolia?" Tom asked.

"No, I thought I would come along this evening in the hope of understanding it. I have a member of my church who's seeking help from me. He says that he's hearing voices from the faces he sees in objects," Alec answered.

"Are you a vicar?" Tom asked.

"No, a pastor - Alec Jackson. This is my wife, Alice," he said. "Have you got time to talk?"

"That's what I do for a living," Tom chuckled. "So what is it you would like to know?"

"I must confess, before this chap came up to me at church, I knew little or nothing about Pareidolia. I can understand a shape resembling a face, but it's the voice bit that concerns me. You mentioned in your talk a little about people hearing words when a record is played backwards, but this chap says that he can have a conversation with the shape. If I didn't know that he was a doctor, I would have probably dismissed it. Have you come across anything like that?" Alec asked.

A smile came across Tom's face.

"You know, Pastor, for years I've been waiting to hear that someone else has experienced that."

"You know of *others*?" Alec said, surprised.

"Not others – myself. And no, Pastor, I'm not possessed, in case you're thinking that," Tom chuckled.

"No, I wasn't thinking that you were. It's just that it's hard to believe that a face (whether on a piece of wood, stone or a vegetable) can possess a life that can *talk*.   In fact, it's totally inconceivable," Alec replied.

"Excuse the pun, Pastor, but, on the face of it, it can't."

"Then how is it possible a person can hear it, unless they are possessed?" Alec asked.

"You believe in the supernatural don't you, Pastor? And a God that says, 'All things are possible to those who believe.'?"

"Yes . . ."

"Well, if a person is open to believe that, what's to say they couldn't believe that a tree (or a stone or whatever) can talk to them? If I remember, didn't God make a donkey speak?"

"Yes. So, are you suggesting that it's God speaking through these objects?" Alec asked, suspiciously.

"Well, if I didn't know what I know now, I would have suggested that (him being God), but no the complete opposite, Pastor."

"I'm sorry, Professor, now you've lost me."

"I think we'd better sit down, as what I'm about to tell you will sound a bit far-fetched to you.

When I was a child I saw my father disappear into a tree and my mother's partner disappear into a stone and, before you say it, it wasn't just a child's imagination. I admit I was on my own with my father when it happened to him, but when my mother's partner disappeared, she was present. Even now, I go back to the tree to talk to my father. In my late teens I promised him I would find a way back for him, and I'm still looking. From what he's told me, he is in another dimension, a place where there's only darkness; he says it's just an empty void of nothingness and torment."

"Sounds like hell, and, if it is, there isn't a way back. The Bible says that there is a great chasm, so that those who want to go between there and heaven cannot," Alec said.

"That might be, Pastor, but where we are is not heaven and I can't believe that my father was that wicked to warrant going where he is. I remember, as a child, asking my mother who the strangers were that he brought home with him. Mother used to say, "That's your father - always helping people and feeding them." So surely, in God's eyes, he doesn't deserve to go there? That's if it *is* hell."

"True — this isn't heaven, and your father sounds as if he was a good man. But we don't get to heaven by doing good things," Alec answered.

"Sorry, Pastor, I'm not into all this religious stuff. To me it's simple: good go to heaven and bad go to hell (that's if you really believe it all)."

"Alec could see that the conversation was making the Professor defensive, which he didn't want as he still hadn't got the answer he he'd come for. Changing the subject, he asked: "Tell me, can anyone else hear when your father talks to you?"

"No. I wish they could, then I could prove after all these years that this other world does exist."

"Do you believe in hell?" Alec asked.

"I've studied the Bible, looking for answers, along with every book and newspaper article on the subject, and still haven't found any. But, having read the Bible, I confess I do believe some of it - about hell."

"Is that only in hell, or that there is a loving God that doesn't want you there?"

"Are you trying to get me 'saved', Pastor?" Tom laughed.

"I wouldn't be doing my job, Professor, if I didn't grasp an opportunity when it came along," Alec replied.

Changing the subject, Tom said: "Would it be possible to meet this doctor chap of yours? I think he might be able to help me."

"I can't see why not, but you will have to come to church."

"Can you not just give me his address?" Tom asked.

"No, I can't. He may not want me to. As I said, come to church and I'll introduce you to him, then you can ask him yourself."

"What time?" Tom replied, reluctantly.

"10.30. So we'll see you there?"

"Where is it, Pastor?"

"Jubilee Christian Fellowship. It's . . ."

Tom looked at his watch and said, "I'm sorry, Pastor, they're waiting to lock up. Just give me the postcode and I'll find it."

On their way home, Alice said: "You can take that smug smile off your face."

"What?"

"You know what. I can't take you anywhere without you trying to get people saved," she replied.

"I am a pastor, Alice! I know he's not saved *yet,* but hopefully after Sunday he will be."

"I was only pulling your leg! Of course you are and a lovely one too," she replied.

Directed by the sat-nav, Tom drove into a school car park. He arrived early and could see only a few parked cars, causing him to think that he was in the wrong place, especially as it was a school and he was looking for a church building. He looked around and couldn't see any signs saying 'Jubilee Christian Fellowship'. He was just about to drive out, when several cars started to come in. He watched the people get out and go round the side of the building, so he decided to follow. He turned the corner and there, above the door, hung the sign. Inside the lobby, waiting to greet him were the pastor and his wife.

"You decided to come then, Professor? So nice to see you," he said with a smile.

Alice held out her hand. "Welcome to our church, Professor Harvey."

I haven't come for church, he said to himself. "Thank you . . .?"

"Alice," she said, shaking his hand.

"Is the doctor chap here?" Tom asked.

"No, not yet, but I should think he will be soon. Why don't you go on in and take a seat," Alec suggested.

Tom made his way through the double doors into a hall and sat at the back so he could keep his eyes on the door. He was hoping the pastor would come in with the chap and introduce him.

The hall soon filled up and Alec went to the front to open the meeting.

I reckon he's deliberately not introduced me to this guy before the meeting so I'll stay, Tom thought to himself.

He soon found himself surrounded by people, singing and clapping their hands to the lively music. The fact that he was the only one still in his seat and not singing made him self-conscious, but on the plus side, it had been a long time since he had nothing to do but sit. The music changed to a slow pace and he noticed that some people were sitting and closing their eyes, soaking it in. That suited him; all he had to do was close his eyes and it wouldn't be obvious that he wasn't one of them.

As he sat there, he experienced a calming effect him from the music. Normally, he could never switch his mind off from his research, but something was happening to him. A sense of peace was coming over him that he had never experienced before. Fifteen minutes ago he was wishing that the meeting would hurry up and end, but now, because of the peace, he wanted more.

The sound of Alec's voice from the front made him open his eyes. He was talking about salvation. Although Tom had come across the subject, reading the Bible occasionally in connection with his research, Alec seemed to speak in a way that was somehow reaching him. Tom's mind was different to most, as he would analyse every word to get an understanding that suited his way of thinking. He found that he had many questions for Alec when the meeting came to an end.

Tom hung around afterwards to talk to Alec. He had come with the sole purpose of meeting a guy to ask him questions, now he was surprised to find that he had what seemed more important questions on the subject of salvation.

"So did you enjoy the meeting?" asked Alec.

"Well, if I were a betting man (which I'm not) I would have put money on me being bored stiff and desperate to get out of here, but I have to be honest: yes, I did. I even have one or two questions for you about what you said," Tom replied.

"Yes? Alec said, with a smile.

"You mentioned that the Bible says that we are all sinners. Surely not *everyone* is? I mean, I know some really good people that do lots of voluntary work."

"I know what you mean, there are some lovely, kind people around. The issue is, though, that we can't do anything to *earn* salvation, however good we try to be. If it worked that way, hardly anyone would make it to heaven – I certainly wouldn't."

"I would have thought that, as long as the good outweighed the bad stuff, it would be okay."

"Try saying that to an earthly judge. Sorry I mugged and robbed that old lady, but I've mowed by neighbour's lawn for him several times and given loads of money to charity. No, we could never be good enough. The Bible says: 'For all have sinned and fallen short of the glory of God."

"So, according to what you were saying earlier, that's why Jesus died - to pay for our sins. If that's the case, surely everyone goes to heaven automatically."

"That's another mistake people make. Jesus died to give us the *gift* of eternal life in heaven. Now, a gift doesn't belong to you until you *accept* it. If you spend your life ignoring the gift that's on offer, it doesn't belong to you."

"Well, *how* do you accept it?"

"You tell him."

"That simple?

"Yes, you tell him you're sorry for the wrong things you've done and thank him for dying on the cross to pay for them. You ask him to be your Lord and Saviour."

Tom scratched his head. "So, that's it? It seems too . . . easy."

"Well, it's the most important decision you could ever make. It determines where you'll spend eternity. Would you like to hear what the Bible has to say?"

Tom looked at his watch. "I'm going to have to get going. Maybe we can continue this another time."

"That's fine, Professor, you know where I am. But didn't you come to meet Dr Martin?"

"That's right, I did. All this has side-tracked me."

Alec looked over Tom's shoulder and could see Dr Martin about to leave.

"Excuse me a minute, Professor; Dr Martin is over there. I'll just grab him before he goes."

Tom turned, to see them talking together. He made his way over.

"Professor Harvey, this is Dr Martin. I think you two have something in common to talk about," Alec said, leaving them together.

"Thank you, Doctor Martin, for being willing to talk to me," Tom said.

"Not at all. It's a relief to have someone who understands what I've experienced. The pastor says that you are an authority on the subject of Pareidolia, and the paranormal?"

"I don't know about an 'authority', as there's still so much I don't know, hence coming here to talk to you. I was hoping I could learn a little more. So, you're a doctor?" Tom said.

"Yes, a neurological surgeon - so you see why I couldn't go around asking anyone for help; they would think *my* brain needed operating on," the doctor chuckled.

"See what you mean. I think we'll have a lot to talk about. By the way, I'm Tom."

"Miles," the doctor replied.

"What about if we exchange numbers and meet up somewhere else? Apart from the fact that everyone has gone, I don't think this is the place we can talk," Tom said.

Chapter Nine

Tom was busy in his study when his phone rang.

"Is that Tom? It's Miles here, Miles Martin. Look I've got a few days off; I was wondering if we could meet up and continue our discussion?"

"Yes - when were you thinking of?"

"Later today (or tomorrow) - if that's not too short notice?" Miles said.

Keen on meeting him, Tom answered: "This afternoon - say about 2.30? You could come here if you like, then I could show you some of my research on the subject."

"2.30 it is. Text me your postcode."

Tom busied himself tidying up his study, and collecting the papers that were scattered all around the room.

At 2.30 on the dot the doorbell rang.

Tom welcomed him in and said, "You're a man after my own heart, Miles."

"How do you mean?"

"Being punctual."

"I have to in my profession. Can you imagine if I was late for an operation?"

"See what you mean. Well, let's go to my study. So, Miles, the pastor tells me that, not only do you see faces, but you have conversations with them?"

"Although I see them, it's only one that I can hear talk," Miles replied.

"So, how old were you when it started?" Tom asked.

"The first time I experienced it was when I was seven. Even before that I was always interested in fine details in objects and shapes, but I remember it well. My parents bought me a microscope for my seventh birthday. Of course I couldn't wait to go out in the garden and fetch something to look at.

It was a piece of old garden vegetation. On first examination, it looked what it was, but when I looked at it under the microscope and zoomed in,

I could see a face. It wasn't just a case of dots for eyes and a line for the mouth; it was detailed in every way, a totally formed face. "Wow!" I said, but what I heard in response to that made the 'wow' seem insignificant. "Yes, I'm real," came a voice from it. I pulled away from the microscope, not believing what I had just heard. Slowly I went back to look again. The face was still there. "Did you just say something?" I said, feeling foolish as I was saying it. "Yes, I said I'm real." Then I asked: "How can you talk?" It said: "Why do you ask such a question? We can all talk." Then I said that a garden leaf couldn't talk. There was a reply: "What's a garden leaf?" I then said: "That's what you are under my microscope." It replied: "I don't understand."

"No, and I can't believe I'm talking to a leaf. Do you have a name?" I said. Well, it didn't understand what a name was and after some explaining, I called it 'Leafy' and told it "I'm Miles". I then asked if there were more like him (or it)?

"And it said, 'Yes'? Tom asked.

"How did you know?" Miles responded.

"Because that's what I found out from my father and Edward."

"How does your father know, and who's Edward?"

"As a child I witnessed my father disappear into a face on a tree. When I became old enough to drive I went back to that tree, and it was on one of those visits that I heard my father's voice. Although I couldn't see him, we were able to talk to each other. I asked many questions about where he was, and, by the way he answered, I could tell that he was struggling with the answers. He seemed to have a problem remembering anything; I even had to remind him of my name. Yet, making visits over a period of time, I found out that there are many of these faces scattered throughout the world."

"Did you manage to find out what kind of place he's in?" Miles asked.

"My father is trapped in a world of darkness and torment with no way back. He said that it's a world where no matter exists, only consciousness. You cannot see or touch anything, and talking is forbidden. He said that all you can hear are the thoughts of the others that still can think, and even those cannot remember much, for when they do, there is unbearable pain for them. It's not long before their minds have been wiped clean. So I have spent my life trying to find a way for him to get back."

"It sounds a nightmare of a place. So who's Edward?" Miles asked.

"Edward is the face on a stone that talked to me when I was a child, and still does. Would you like to see him? It would be interesting to see if you can hear him talk."

"Yes it would be," Miles agreed.

Tom went over to fetch the stone, which was sitting on top of the filing cabinet.

"Are you there, Edward?"

"Yes, I'm here. I have been listening to what he has been saying."

"Will he be able to hear you?" Tom asked.

"No, only you can. I think that's how it works; each of us seems to be assigned to one person, for some reason."

"Then what about my father? He can hear me and I can hear him?"

"Yes, strange that, Tom. I have no answer."

"Tom," Miles interjected, "I can only hear *you* talking."

"Yes, Edward says that apparently only the ones who find them can hear them. It seems that's the way it is in their world."

"Interesting. I heard you say something about the fact that you can hear your father as well. What did he reply to that?"

"He didn't have an answer."

"So at least we have found out a little more about the strange world of Pareidolia. Have you

83

come up with any theories on why, or how, the likes of you and me can see and hear them?"

"There's probably many more like us out there; they're probably too scared to come forward, in case people think they're insane. Who knows the answer, Miles? I'm just thankful I know someone else who experiences it."

"Me too."

"Has 'Leafy' ever spoken to you about what they call 'gathering'?" Tom asked.

"No; what's that?"

"Apparently, it's their sole purpose - to gather people from this world into theirs."

"Did your father tell you that?" Miles asked.

"No, Edward told me; it was a question I once asked him, having witnessed my father and my mother's partner disappearing."

"How many have you witnessed?"

"Just the two, thankfully." (Tom didn't want to include the school bully as, now that he was older, he felt ashamed of his part in it.)

"So how come *we* haven't been gathered?" Miles asked.

"You know, I've never asked that question, Miles."

"Why don't you ask Edward then? Would he tell you?"

"There's only one way to find out. Edward, why haven't you gathered me?"

"Sorry, Tommy, I don't know. All I know is, there's something special about you that stops me, and anyway I don't think I want to. Gordon feels it as well," Edward replied.

"How's he doing? I went to the tree the other day but he wasn't there," Tom said.

"I think he's getting more distant every time we speak. Tommy, I don't think his mind will last much longer unless you somehow get him out."

"I'm trying Edward. Can you tell him not to give up - I *will* bring him home."

"What are you trying to do, Tommy?" Edward replied, sounding confused. "Sorry - I think the darkness has been listening in. It's wiping my memory; I'm struggling to keep with you. I can't .."

"Edward, are you there? Don't go - I need you to stay with me!" Tom said, alarmed.

"Everything all right, Tom?" Miles asked.

"Yeah, it's Edward. He's been prevented from talking to me. It happens every now and then, especially if I ask questions," Tom replied.

"If these faces are all over the world, and their sole purpose is to gather people into their realm, then there must be thousands of people over time (if not millions) that have been gathered there. Surely someone in authority must be asking questions about why so many are disappearing and where they've gone?" Miles questioned.

"And as there is no way back for those who have been taken, they will never know. That's why, if I can somehow get my father back, we might have a chance of letting them know what's going on right under their noses, but its easier said then done. And even if it were possible, would they believe us? You know you're not too far wrong there, Miles - about the amount. There have been millions upon millions over the years that have disappeared. I have a theory that the authorities just assume that either they don't want to be found, or that they've been murdered and buried somewhere. Some are attributed to abduction.

A lot of them are found, either alive or dead. It's the ones that are never found that I've been doing the main research on. I reckon they are the ones who are gathered into the world of Pareidolia. The Internet is full of unexplained stories of people that have disappeared and have never been seen again. I know a lot of them, especially the old ones. They get exaggerated over time, but I have investigated several recent cases in person and I have no reason to doubt the authenticity of any of them.

One such story was of a group of businessmen travelling north on an overnight non-stop sleeper train. They had all been eating and drinking in the diner car when a chap called Bill Watson said to the others that he was going to retire. That was the last they saw of him. When he didn't meet the others for breakfast, they thought he had overslept. One of the group went to his sleeping car. He found that the clothes Bill was wearing the night before were at the side of his bed, including his wallet, but there was no sign of Bill. They searched the train from one end to the other, but he had simply vanished. As the train was a non-stop, it was impossible for him to have got off. I wanted to investigate further by checking out the actual carriage he was in, but trying to get the authorities to let me on the train while it was in the sidings wasn't easy. However, it's amazing what a bit of money will do. Having entered the carriage, my suspicions were right. The first thing I noticed on the upholstery was the swirling pattern, in which I could see a multitude of faces."

"You're saying they took him?" Miles said.

"Knowing what they can do, there's no other explanation as far as I'm concerned. There's another recent case I investigated, of the strange disappearance of a woman's husband. It was their anniversary and they had decided to have some drinks at a local bar. They had been there most of the evening, having a nice time together. Before they left, the husband said that he wanted to use the toilet. His wife saw him go in. After some time, she became concerned that maybe he was unwell, and asked the bartender to go in and check. When he returned, he reported that there was no one in there. She told me it was impossible for him to have come out without her noticing, as the only door to the toilet was in full view of their table. The security camera footage showed him entering but not actually leaving. With no evidence of foul play or any reason for his disappearance, I had to go there and check out the place for myself. The first thing I looked for were any patterns in the upholstery or carpets of the bar, but there were none. The upholstery was plain black vinyl and the floor was wood laminate with no swirling grains in the wood. That left the toilets to investigate. The first thing I noticed was that there were no windows that he might have climbed out. Then I noticed that the tiles all around were patterned. Suspecting that somewhere in the random patterns there could possibly be a face (or faces), I started to search. There were none around the urinals, so I looked in each of the cubicles. As I opened the door of the furthest one, there on the back wall was a face in the pattern. I concluded that he must have used that cubicle."

"But surely, Tom, that cubical must have been used by others, like the train carriage, and if everyone who used them disappeared it would be well known."

"That's the mystery, Miles. Not everyone who looks upon them is taken."

"They might be looking at them, but maybe they don't see the faces. It could be that it's only those whose brains decipher the patterns as faces that are taken."

"That's a good theory, Miles. It might explain it," he said, taking notes.

"Well, Tom the brain *is* my subject," he said with a grin. "I often wonder at how amazingly complex the human brain is. Along with performing millions of mundane acts, it composes concertos, issues manifestos and comes up with elegant solutions to equations. It has feelings, behaviours, experiences as well as being the repository of memory and self-awareness. So it's no surprise that the brain remains a mystery to us."

"Is it true that we only use ten percent of our brains?" Tom asked.

"Though an alluring idea, the "10 percent myth" is so wrong it's almost laughable. Evidence would show that over a day we use 100 percent of the brain. Ultimately, it's not that we use 10 percent of our brains, merely that we only understand about 10 percent of how it functions," Miles answered.

"So we're still no closer to understanding why the likes of you and I can communicate with the Pareidolia world," Tom sighed.

"It appears not, Tom."

Miles looked at his watch.

"I think I'm going to have to leave it there, Tom. I've got stuff I must get on with."

"Of course; maybe we can continue another day?"

"I was hoping you would say that. By the way, if we don't meet up before Sunday, will I see you at church?

"I'm not sure, Miles, but say hello to the pastor for me if not."

"Will do. I'll ring you if I don't see you," Miles replied.

Chapter Ten

"**S**orry I didn't get to see how your meeting with Professor Harvey went last Sunday," the pastor said to Miles.

"Oh, we only chatted briefly, but we met up during the week. It was very interesting."

"Good. I think I would have liked to have been there. Since attending his lecture, I can't stop thinking about the subject," Alec replied.

"I tell you what, Pastor, we're going to meet up again this week. How about coming along? I think you'd be an asset to the discussion."

"Shouldn't you check with the professor first?"

"I'm sure it will be okay, but I'll mention it to him. Anyway he might turn up here yet, then I'll ask him.

"I must confess I was hoping he would," the Alec replied.

"That was a good meeting, Pastor Alec."

"Thank you, Miles. It was a shame the professor didn't come."

"I know, maybe he will in the future," Miles replied.

"I'll pray for him. Say hello from me when you see him."

"Will do, Pastor Alec."

"Tom, Miles here. Are you free Thursday?"

"If I rescheduled a few things I can be. Same time?" Tom answered.

"Sure. By the way, I was speaking to the pastor on Sunday. He wondered if he could come along. What do you think?"

"Could be a good idea to have another viewpoint," Tom replied.

"That's what I was thinking. If it has something to do with some dark evil force, then what better than to have a pastor on board? So, I'll bring him along then."

"I'll be looking forward to it - there's something I want to run past you," Tom replied.

"It sounds ominous. Can you not tell me now?" Miles asked.

"No, I'll wait until we're all together."

"Okay Tom, we'll see you Thursday.

"Come on in," Tom said, showing them into his study.

"I hope you don't mind me gate-crashing," the pastor said.

"No, on the contrary, I'm glad you're here."

"So, Tom, what was it that you wanted to run past us?" Miles asked.

"Before I tell you, I want you to promise me you won't try and talk me out of it."

"How can we promise you when we don't know what it is, Tom?" Miles said.

"Well, it doesn't matter if you do. I've made up my mind."

"Professor, why don't you just tell us?" Pastor Alec said.

"I'm going to try and cross over into their world," Tom announced.

"Are you *mad*, Tom? Didn't you tell me there's no way back?" Miles said, alarmed.

"I know I did, but I've run out of answers and this way is the only way I'll get them."

"But what's the point, if you can't get back with them?" Miles asked.

"I'm not going there without a plan. I intend coming back, and bringing my father, as I promised him."

"Are you forgetting one thing, Tom? There's something about you and me that stops us from going there, so even if we were with you in this madness, you can't," Miles said.

"I've already told Edward what I intend to do and asked him for his help to make it possible."

"What did he say?" Miles asked.

"He said he didn't know for sure, but maybe the reason is that he didn't *want* to gather me (and my father didn't either). But if someone else gathered me, it might happen."

"Pastor, you haven't said anything yet. What's do *you* think about it?" Miles said, turning to him.

"Firstly, can I ask who Edward is?" the pastor asked.

"Edward is Tom's stone - it talks to him, Pastor," Miles responded.

"A *stone*?"

"Don't ask, Pastor," Miles said, chuckling.

94

"How can I comment when I don't know understand anything about it?" Pastor Alec said.

Tom filled him in on all that he knew.

"So now that you know, Pastor, what do you think? Is the place evil?" Tom asked.

The pastor sat there thinking, then he said, "I would say: yes, Professor, and let me tell you why I think that. You told me that your father described it as a place of darkness, nothingness and torment. As I said at the time, it sounds like hell. We know from the Bible that there are such things as demons. Their purpose is to take people to hell when they die (by keeping them from accepting salvation). s they are opening a portal between them and us. I think you have already called it a 'dimension'."

"So you are saying my father has gone to hell? Well, he told me there are children there. How does that work then, Pastor?" Tom asked, raising his voice.

"I don't mean to upset you again, Professor - about your father and why he's there (or the children). I haven't got any answers. We have to look at all the angles on this, if you are adamant about going there."

To break the tension, Miles said, "Tom, tell us how you propose to do it?"

"Miles, seeing you're a surgeon, can you lay your hands on a defibrillator, electroencephalograph and a electrocardiogram?" Tom asked him.

"I know what a defibrillator is but what are the others?" the pastor enquired.

"An electroencephalograph is to record electrical activity of the brain (EEG for short). An electrocardiogram (also known by the abbreviations: ECG and EKG) detects low-voltage electrical activity of the heart through electrodes placed on the chest, Pastor," Miles explained. "So I take it, Tom, from what you are asking, you're going there wired up?"

"That's the thing, Miles, if the machines are not wireless, I'm thinking that any wire attached to me might break or something, not knowing what's on the other side. But the question is, are they available, or are there even such things?"

"I know the defibrillator unit is, but the pads have wires attached. Although, that's not to say there aren't any, and I'm pretty sure there must be a wireless version of a electroencephalograph, but again I will find out if I can get my hands on wireless electrodes. You seem to have put a lot of thought into this, Tom."

"Better safe than sorry," Tom chuckled.

"Tom, this is no laughing matter. We are dealing with the unknown. The minute you step over into that world, you'll be on your own."

"No, I won't Miles. Your machines will be monitoring me, and not only that, I'm proposing to have wireless communication. Pastor, do you know how to operate a video camera?"

"Well . . . I suppose so - yes, why?"

"We'll be documenting it all the way. It will be the proof I need to show the existence of this world of Pareidolia," Tom said excitedly.

"I still say this is madness, Tom; in fact it's suicidal!" Miles exclaimed.

"Madness it might be, Miles, but I wouldn't go as far as to call it suicidal; I'm not some manic depressive with a death wish."

"I know you're not, Tom; it's a figure of speech - emphasizing the seriousness of what you want to do," Miles said.

"What do you think, Pastor, do you think it's suicidal? And if I go ahead, knowing the risk, would God consider it suicide? And if so, where would I end up?"

"That's a good question, Professor. The Bible does have accounts of people who committed suicide, but it doesn't say where their souls went, to heaven or to hell. But, Jesus promised: "I am the resurrection and the life – he who believes in

97

me, though he may die – yet shall he live. That's in John 11:25."

"So it sounds like I have to safeguard myself before committing suicide, Miles," Tom chuckled.

"Okay - I wish I never used the word," Miles replied. "So can we get serious here? Where and when are you intending to try to go there?"

"As soon as you can get hold of the equipment. I've been thinking about attempting it either here in my study, or at the tree. The trouble is though: if I go in via Edward's stone (in my office), will I be anywhere near my father? I don't even know if I'd be near him if went in via the tree, but as it's the place where he disappeared and where I've talked to him, it's the more likely of the two."

"I assume this tree is in a public place?" Pastor Alec asked.

"It is, but it's not really a place that you would choose to go to. The only reason my father found it was because I had a call of nature. No, I shouldn't think

anyone will be around, but to make sure, we should go there as soon as it gets light in the morning. That should ensure no one will see what we're up to," replied Tom.

"So, what day?" Miles said.

"As I said, it's all down to when you can come up with the equipment," Tom said.

"If I can get hold of the equipment tomorrow, what about Saturday morning? Or is that too soon for everyone?" Miles said.

"For me, sooner the better," Tom replied.

"And you, Pastor?" Miles asked.

"I did have something on for Saturday, but I'm sure a phone call will sort it. Do we know whether it's going to be wet?"

"Good point, Pastor. That's the last thing we want on the equipment," Miles replied.

"It's going to be fine. I heard it this morning on the radio," Tom announced.

"If you don't mind me asking, Doc, are you just going to walk out with all that stuff?" the pastor asked.

"Don't worry, Pastor. I'm not stealing it, - just borrowing it. I'll have it back by Monday, and no one will even notice that it's been used. Anyway, I don't even know at this point if the machines have the requirements we need."

"I wasn't suggesting that you were going to steal it; it's just that I can't see how someone can walk out with all that valuable equipment."

"I'm not just someone, Pastor, I'm a senior surgeon, and no one would even question it (that's if they saw me)."

"Okay, it's settled. So I take it that you will help me?" Tom said.

Miles looked at the pastor, who shook his head and said, "What choice do we have?"

Deep inside, Pastor Sean was concerned for Tom's soul. He knew he couldn't voice his concerns to Tom, as he felt sure he wouldn't want to know. The problem was - he only had tomorrow to get close to him.

"Tom, would you like to have a meal with my wife and me tomorrow night - nothing formal, just a relaxed evening, good food in good company?" the pastor asked, hoping that somehow he'd be able to get on the subject of salvation.

"What - like the last supper?" Tom chuckled.

Miles laughed.

"As I said, Tom - just good food and company. So what do you say?"

"I must confess, Pastor, it would make a change for me – from eating take-aways on my own."

"So, that's a yes?"

"As long as there's no preaching."

"I'll tell you what, I'll won't mention the word 'God' unless you want me to," the pastor chuckled.

"What time then?" Tom replied.

"7, o'clock. Does that suit you?"

Chapter Eleven

Tom turned up on time with a bottle of wine in his hand.

"Welcome to my home, Tom!   Come on in."

"I hope you drink red wine," Tom said, handing the bottle to him.

"Oh sorry, Tom, we don't drink."

"I'm sorry. I should have realised - you being a pastor."

"No, its not because we're pastors; it's just our preference not to, but please, we have no objection to you having a glass."

"The truth is, Pastor, I've been trying to give It up for years. I know I drink far too much, but I just find I can't."

"In your own strength it's hard, but with the Lord you will find you can."

"You preaching, Pastor?"

"Sorry, Tom. It's natural for me to say such things. Look, we'd better go and sit down. Alice will have the food on the table and one thing you don't do is keep a woman waiting to serve her meal," he laughed.

"Hello, Tom. It's so nice that you could come," Alice said.

"How could I refuse a home-cooked meal, Pastor Alice?" Tom replied with a smile.

"Tom, let's do away with the formalities - Alice and Alec will be fine. That's all right with you, dear, isn't it?" she said, looking at her husband.

"Of course! Right, do you mind if I give thanks for the food, Tom, or will you think I'm preaching?" he chuckled.

"Alec!" his wife said, giving him a look.

"Tom knows I'm joking, dear. Isn't that right, Tom?"

"Sure. That's all right, Pastor; I mean, Alec - of course," Tom said.

Having finished their meal, Alice said, "Alec, why don't you take Tom in the other room while I clear away."

"I just want to say, Alice, that was some meal you cooked! I haven't had food like that since I left home as a youngster. Any chance, Alec, that I can borrow her?" Tom said, chuckling.

"Well thank you, Tom. You hear that, dear? Someone appreciates me," she said to her husband.

"I always appreciate you and your cooking. You see, Tom, that's what having a good woman in your life does. I take it there's no woman in yours?" Alec asked him.

"No woman and no family, I'm afraid; as I've dedicated my life to getting my father home, it just never happened for me."

"I take it your mother isn't around anymore then?" Alec asked.

"No, she passed away about a year ago," Tom replied.

"I'm sorry to hear that, Tom," Alice said. "Would you like some coffee?"

"Yes, black - no sugar, thank you."

"Alec, take Tom in; I'll be there in a minute with the coffees."

"So Tom, I know that you've dedicated your time to your father, but do you find time to travel?" Alec asked.

"What, like holidays?" he replied.

"Holidays, travelling in connection with your work? Anything like that?"

"I can't remember when I last had a holiday, but sometimes I have to travel abroad lecturing."

"And do you take out travel insurance?"

"Of course I do. Well, I don't personally – it's paid for by the university when they send me."

"So it's a free gift?" Alec asked.

"A perk that comes with the job – yes; but even if they didn't I would make sure I had it. It would be crazy not to, you never know what can happen. You could have an accident, become sick, or even die. Why do you ask? Don't tell me you're an insurance salesman in your spare time?" Tom laughed.

"Then would you agree that insurance gives you peace of mind?"

"I suppose it does," Tom replied.

"Okay Tom, bear with me. What if you were to die abroad without that insurance; what do you think would happen to you?"

"I haven't a clue; then does anyone think about it? Would it worry me?"

"Probably not, but it should do. What about the loved one you've left behind? Would you want them to worry about how they are going to bring you home?"

"That wouldn't apply to me - I haven't got any; as far as I'm concerned, they can bury me in a ditch."

"There must be someone who cares for you?"

"No, not really."

"What, you haven't even got a friend?"

"Well, of course I've got friends, but why would they want to fork out money for me? Why would anyone?"

"I would, if I was to hear about it."

"What – you'd pay money to bring me home?"

"Yes, Tom, I would."

"But why? You don't really know me."

"I wouldn't be doing it for you, Tom. I'd be doing it for the Lord. He says, 'Truly I tell you, whatever you did for one of the least of these brothers and sisters of mine, you did for me.' You see, Tom, Jesus cares about you. He doesn't want anything bad to happen to you, especially if you were to die."

"So that's what this is really about! And I thought there for a moment you were going to sell me travel insurance. Very clever, Pastor," Tom said.

Alice came in, carrying a tray of coffees.

"Here, let me take that," Tom said, standing up.

"Thank you, Tom. So what've you two been talking about?" Alice asked.

"Your husband has been trying to sell me travel insurance," Tom replied.

"Travel insurance!" Alice exclaimed, baffled.

"I've been asking Tom if he travelled a lot, that's all - and if he has travel insurance, as none of us know what lies ahead. Now, if you'll excuse me, I must go to the bathroom."

Alice twigged what her husband was leading up to with Tom, so she asked, "And do you, Tom?"

"Yes, Alice, I do. But if you are really asking if I'm sure that if I were to die I wouldn't go to hell, then the answer would be 'no'. Alec was telling me that if I became ill abroad without insurance, he would get me home. I asked him why he would do that for me."

"And what did he say?" Alice said.

"He told me he would be doing it for the Lord."

"That's right, Tom, he would be. You see He gave Tom a heart of compassion for people. You know, I've seen Alec come home without shoes, and when I asked him why, he said that he saw a man who had no shoes because he couldn't afford them; so he gave the man his. I know he's my husband, but that's the type of man he is and I know if he had to give his life for a friend he wouldn't hesitate."

"What would make him do something like that? I know I couldn't," Tom said.

"It's because Jesus lives in his heart, Tom, and because of that he has such a passion for saving souls, so I won't make excuses for him trying to save you."

"He comes across as being passionate," Tom replied.

"Yes, and he doesn't want your soul to be lost, Tom. He was trying to say that, if you die without knowing the Lord Jesus, you will end up in hell. Are you prepared to take that risk, Tom?"

"Well, no."

"Then let me lead you in a prayer to save you from going there," Alice said.

"Would it please you and Alec if I let you?"

"I don't want you to please us - although it would make us happy. We want you to do it for yourself. It's not just spouting words into the air. You have to mean it - it has to come from your heart, Tom."

"Alice, I've never said or done anything I've not meant. Don't worry - it will come from my heart. Now what do I have to do?"

"Just say this prayer, and by the way, this 'insurance' is a free gift from the Lord."

"Lord Jesus, I come to you and confess that I am a sinner, that I have lied, thought evil in my heart, and have broken your Word. Please forgive me of my sins. I trust in what you have done on the cross and I receive you. Please cleanse me of my sin and be the Lord of my life. I trust you completely for the forgiveness of my sins and put no trust in my own efforts of righteousness. Lord Jesus, please save me."

Alec came back in, to see Tom and Alice hugging. "Hello, what's going on here then? I think hugging might be a bit over the top for my wife's cooking, Tom."

"Your wife's cooking is worth more than that, Alec," Tom said, chuckling.

"He's one of the family now," Alice announced.

"Welcome to the family, Tom! Now I can relax about what you are intending to do tomorrow."

"Is that what all this was about, Alec?" Tom said.

"No, not just because of tomorrow; it's the Lord's desire that all men should know him."

"So, tell me Alec, what has travel insurance to do with tomorrow?"

"Everything, Tom. Are you not going on a journey, not knowing what might happen to you, where you might even die?"

"You said you wouldn't preach, Alec, and now I find myself being saved."

"All I said was that I wouldn't use the word 'God' and I didn't."

"Very good, Alec, ten out of ten. You two should start a company called the AA."

"If I'm not mistaken, there's already a company with that name who deal with breakdown and recue?"

"Precisely what you two do: rescue people who've broken down," Tom said.

"Very good, Tom, but why AA?"

"Alec and Alice," Tom laughed. "Well you two, I have an early start in the morning and so have you, Alec; that's if you're still coming?"

"Of course I am."

"Well, thank you for the food and the company; I'll say goodnight. Oh, and thanks for selling me the 'insurance', Alec."

"You're welcome," Alec replied.

"Goodnight, Tom; we'll do it again. I'll pray for you tomorrow," Alice said.

While the pair of them were lying in bed, reading, Alice said, "Should I be concerned about you tomorrow?"

"It's not me you should be concerned about, it's Tom. He's the one venturing into the unknown.

Rest assured, I will be keeping my distance from that tree he mentioned," Alec replied.

"Make sure you do, I don't know what I'd do if something happened to you."

"Even if something did happen, you must take comfort that the Lord will be with me, Alice."

"I know I shouldn't concern myself over it, but it still won't stop me from praying."

"That's what we are called to do, Alice, and I wouldn't want you to stop. Now can I get on with reading my book?"

Chapter Twelve

"How much further is this place, Tom?"

"Just around the next bend on the left. This is it! Just pull up on the verge," Tom replied.

"It's a bit chilly and damp out here," the pastor said, getting out and doing his coat up.

"It's only the morning air; it will soon pass," Tom said, starting to unload Miles' car.

"Where now, Tom?" Miles asked.

"Through these trees here and a little way in; follow me."

"Good - this stuff is heavy," grunted the pastor.

"This is it," Tom said, placing some of the equipment down.

"So where's this tree?" Miles enquired.

"It's the big one over there," Tom said, pointing.

"I see what you mean about the face - it's so detailed," he said walking over towards it.

"Stop, Miles! It might not be safe for you," Tom cried out.

Miles stopped in his tracks. "Do you think it will take me then?"

"I don't know, but we shouldn't take any chances. That would be the last thing we'd want - to lose you," Tom replied.

"You know, guys, for the love of me I can't see a face - just bark," the pastor said.

"You should count your blessings, Pastor. Our research suggests that it's only those whose brains see the patterns as faces that are in danger of being taken," Miles explained.

"If you say so," Alec replied.

"What do you think the range is, or the signal is from the machines to the electrodes?" Tom asked Miles.

"About six meters; is that long enough?"

"I was hoping it was longer, but it will have to do. As nothing has happened to us, I should think this distance from the tree is safe to set the equipment up. What do you think?" Tom asked.

"I suppose so. We're dabbling with the unknown; either way, we're going to find out shortly," Miles replied.

Tom stood there as if he was looking for something.

"Lost something, Tom?" Miles asked.

"Yes, one of the bags; it must still be in the car. If you let me have your keys, I'll pop back and get it. While I'm gone, don't go near the tree."

"You've already told us, Tom," Miles answered.

The pastor stood there looking at the tree. "Hey Doc, I think I can see the face now. It's amazing how, if you look at it long enough, it appears."

"Now you can see it, make sure you keep this safe distance," Miles warned him.

"Don't worry about that. I have no intention of going to that place, wherever it is," Alec replied.

"So, Pastor, Tom tells me he enjoyed the meal with you and Alice last night. I could see a real difference in him – he's much more calm and relaxed. Did you have a chance to talk to him about salvation?"

"We offered him the opportunity – and he took it."

"So he did! Thank God for that. What would we do without pastors?"

"And doctors, Miles. We both save lives when you think about it."

Tom came back carrying a bag.

"So what's in the bag, Tom?"

"Belts and braces, Pastor."

Not knowing what he meant, the pair carried on setting up the equipment. Then Miles said:

"Right, Tom, if you could come over here, I need to attach all the electrodes, sensors and pads to you."

As soon as he'd finished, Miles announced: "I'm switching on, to check the equipment is working properly - if you could stand still for me?"

The machines gave Tom's heartbeat and brain activity readings. It showed that they were normal, which suggested to Miles that Tom wasn't experiencing any anxiety whatsoever.

"Everything alright, Miles?" Tom asked.

"Under the circumstances, yes."

"Good. Is the camera working, Pastor?"

"Yes."

"Can we try out the two-way radio?" Tom said, speaking into the microphone.

"That's fine, Tom; everything seems to be fine," Miles said.

"There's one more thing. Pastor, in my bag you'll find a nylon rope and a belt. Can you bring it over here?" Tom asked him.

The pastor opened Tom's bag and found the rope and belt. "What are these for?" he asked.

"As I said, belt and braces. Put the belt around my waist, and make sure it's tight. Now tie the other end around that tree over there."

The pastor did as Tom said and gave a tug on the rope. Satisfied with the knot, he said, "I'm happy with that, it would hold a wild horse."

"I'm not worried about any horse, as long as it's strong enough that you two can pull me back - if you have to," Tom said.

"Are you sure you want to go ahead with this? It's not too late to change your mind, Tom," the pastor asked him.

"Yes, I'm sure. I'm ready," Tom replied.

"Then there's only one thing left to do," the pastor said.

"What's that?" Tom said, surprised.

"I'm going to pray for your protection, and that you will come back."

The pastor said a short prayer over Tom.

"If you don't make it back, Tom, I just want to say that it was nice knowing you," Miles said, shaking his hand.

"Oh, thanks for the words of encouragement, Miles."

"That's great! I've just prayed, Doc, that he will come back. Remind me later to talk to you about faith," the pastor said.

"I was just saying!" Miles said, sheepishly.

Tom slowly made his way towards the tree, stopping a meter away from it. He turned to look at the others. Miles noticed the reading levels were still normal.

"Well, here goes!" he said gingerly, reaching out to touch the tree.

"Stop, Tom! Don't do it!" *Was that the voice of his father?*

Recognising the voice, Tom said," Dad . . . I'm coming to get you."

"No, you have to go! I'm being pulled away. There are others here that will gather you if you touch the tree. Don't do it - there is no way back!"

Toms finger was only centimetres from it.

"I don't believe that, Dad! I *want* them to gather me - it's the only way I can help you."

"You're not listening! There is no way back . . . back . . . back," his voice echoed and faded.

Tom shut his eyes and touched the tree. He could feel a floating sensation go through his body as he was drawn into the tree.

Not believing their eyes, Miles and Alec watched as Tom's body disappeared into the tree. The slack on the rope attached to him instantly went taught.

"Doc, the rope - it's breaking!" the pastor shouted.

The two of them watched as slowly the outer coating of the nylon fibres started to break.

"Do you think it will hold?" the pastor said, anxiously.

"I don't know, but if it snaps we will lose him! Whatever he's got to do, he'd better do it quickly," Miles replied.

"Whom was he talking to?" the pastor asked.

"Probably his father; this is where he communicates with him," Miles replied.

"What reading do you have on the machines?"

"They're off the scale, Pastor. His brain must be frying! What can you see on the camera?"

"Nothing - just darkness."

"Is it working?"

"Yes. It's recording a thick darkness," the pastor said, not being able to take his eyes away from the monitor.

"Try speaking to him," Miles said.

"Tom, are you okay?"

There was only silence.

"Anything, Pastor?"

"No, I'll try again. Tom, speak to us! Say something, so we know you're okay."

A loud, high-pitched, hissing sound came from the speaker, followed by what sounded like a scream, which made the two of them cover their ears.

"What was *that*?" the pastor said.

"I don't know! I think it was some kind of high-frequency static."

"That scream wasn't; do you think it was Tom?"

"I hope not!   It sounds like an awful place to be."

"It sounds like hell to me. I pray to God it's not, for Tom's sake."

"I just don't know how to help him, Pastor. I feel so helpless, just standing here."

"You can't.   Only God can."

Chapter Thirteen

Opening his eyes, Tom found there was nothing but complete darkness all around him and an eerie silence.

"Dad, you there?" There was no reply. "Dad it's me T . . ."

Tom couldn't understand why his mind was suddenly confused over his name and how he'd got to wherever he was. As if he was watching a computer screen and someone had their finger on the delete button, fragments of faces and names were flashing before him and fading into the darkness, but the name 'Edward' seemed to want to come from his mouth.

"Edward!" he called out.

"Is that you, Gordon?"

"I don't know. Am I Gordon?" Tom replied.

"I think I'm Gordon," another voice called back.

"Then if you're Gordon, who's is the other voice calling me?" Edward answered.

"I . . . I don't know who I am, or why I said your name," Tom said.

"Edward, it's me – Gordon; that voice seems familiar somehow."

"It does to me, but I'm struggling to think why. Hey, new voice, keep talking. The sound of your voice might remind us who you are."

"Why can't I even remember my name?" Tom replied.

"That's what being here does; you have to concentrate if you want to remember anything, but be quick about it, or you'll lose it all," Edward called back.

Tom's mind hurt as he tried with all his might to think who he was.

"Wow, Pastor, take a look at this needle - his brain activity is spiking off the graph! I think he's struggling with something," Miles said.

"How's his heart rate?" Pastor Alec asked.

"Strangely enough, it's almost flat-lining."

"Well at least it's telling us he's still alive, thank God."

"I think we have to thank your prayers for that. Why don't we try and communicate with him again?"

"Tom, it's me - Pastor Alec; can you hear me?" There was no reply, only static.

"Let me try," Miles said, taking hold of the microphone.

"Tom, . . . Tom! It's me – Miles. If you're unable to talk back and you can hear my voice, give us some sort of sign."

From the speaker came the usual static sound. Miles' eyes went to the monitors, to see that the needle was making a uniform pattern on the graph.

"I think he's responding!" Miles said, excitedly.

"Praise God!" replied the pastor.

Hearing the word 'Tom', reactivated his memory. "I'm Tom. It's me, Dad, Tom! I've come to get . . .". Before Tom could finish his sentence, a wave of vibration shot through him.

"Tom! Oh, *why* did you do it? I told you not to. Edward, it's Tom, my son!"

"What - my friend, Tommy?" Edward replied.

"Yes! He made it here."

"But how, Gordon? I didn't gather him."

"I know, Edward. The last thing I remember was telling him to go, then I was brought back. I'm sure it wasn't me."

"Are you certain, Gordon?"

There was silence, then the words, "Edward, now I'm not sure. I can't remember. Speak to me, Tom, if you can," his father said.

"Dad . . . what's happening to me? There's unbearable pain! It's shaking every molecule of my brain. I can't think."

"It's the darkness, Tom; you have to fight it!"

The place started to shake with such force that it was filled with screams that seemed to go on forever. When it subsided, all that could be heard was the pitiful sound of moaning.

"Pastor, we have a problem! Tom's vitals are dead."

"No . . . that can't be! Are you sure it's not the batteries?"

"I made sure they were new, and as they're capable of running these machines for twenty-four hours, I can't believe it's that," replied Miles.

"Doc, if he was here and his heart stopped, wouldn't we be doing CPR or putting that defibrillator on him to kick-start his heart?"

"But he's *not* here, Pastor."

"I know that, Doc, but what if we somehow send an electric shock to the pads attached to his chest? Would it work?"

"It's a long shot, Pastor, but I suppose it's worth a try."

"Amen there, Doc. It's better than doing nothing, but whatever we do, we have to do it quickly," Alec urged.

"Pastor, in my bag there's a screwdriver; pass it to me, will you?"

Miles took the lid off the defibrillator and studied the circuits, while Alec looked on.

"Do you know what you're doing, Doc?"

"To be honest, Pastor, no. All I know is: I have to get it right first time. I'm connecting the heart cable direct to the power source terminals, to send all the power to his heart. If he's not dead already, this could kill him. Pray, Pastor."

"I already have."

Miles reassembled the unit, hoping he'd got it right.

"This is it, Pastor; let's hope your prayers are answered," he said, as he threw the switch.

A surge of electricity shot down the transmitter. Miles' eyes went to the monitor. A green blip shot up on the screen then went flat.

"Why did you turn it off?"

"I didn't.   We have to try again," Miles announced.

Miles reset the machine to charge and threw the switch. Both sets of eyes were now looking at the monitor. The green blip once again shot up followed by a disappointing flat line.

"Pastor, I think we've lost him."

"No, Doc. You might give up, but I'm not. Shock him again."

Miles didn't argue.   Even though he felt it was futile, he recharged the machine.

"Ready?"

"Do it, Doc. I know it's going to work this time!"

"Miles threw the switch once again. The green blip spiked upwards, followed by a line of slow rhythmic blips going across the screen.

"We've done it, Pastor! We've done it!" Miles said, excitedly.

"It wasn't us, Doc, or the power from the defibrillator. It was a power from above."

"Well, I'll not argue with that! The main thing is, we got him back," Miles said.

"Tommy, it's me – Edward; are you okay? Can you speak?"

"I thought I was on my own there for a moment, Edward. What was that?"

"It was the darkness; it does that when the balance of order is being upset here."

"What do you mean 'balance of order'?"

"There's not supposed to be any talking. You see all those who are gathered here have their minds wiped, so there shouldn't be anything to talk about. The fact that it can hear talking, is telling the darkness that something is wrong, so it sends a wave of vibration to correct it."

"How come you and Dad still remember things?"

"I still do forget, but Gordon helps me to remember things – as I do him. The darkness doesn't like it. How Gordon keeps going, I don't know, as it keeps hitting him with vibrations."

"Can he hear us talking?" Tom asked.

"Who, the darkness?" Edward said.

"No, Dad."

"That last wave was strong. As I said, I don't know how much more he can take without giving in to it. Maybe he is weak at the moment and needs time to recover. So how did you get here?"

"I think I had help; it seems so distant," Tom replied.

"Tommy, you have to remember – if you're to get back! I think I heard you say to Gordon it was the tree, or did you tell me?"

"Tree? Yes - the tree! Miles and the . . pastor. That's it - they're my friends, out there by the tree. We had a plan." Tom started to think. "Yes, I should be able to hear them and they should be able to hear me. Miles, can you hear me?"

"Did you hear that, Doc? I'm sure I heard your name amongst the static!" Pastor Alec exclaimed.

"Are you sure?"

"It sounded like your name. I'm pretty sure. Maybe we'll hear it again."

"I'm not waiting, Pastor! Give me the microphone. Tom! Are you trying to communicate? If you are, say something."

"Miles, it's me. I can hear you. Thank God you're there!"

Tom's voice was broken up by interference.

"Tom, I'm only getting fragments of your voice. What did you say?"

"I'm here; I can hear you!"

Miles and Alec waited intently for Tom's voice. Instead of the usual intermittent static in the speaker, it was now continuous.

"I think we've lost him, Pastor. It just seems like he's so far away."

126

"Were you talking to your friends?" Edward asked.

"Yes, but there's so much interference stopping me."

"It's where we are, Tom," Edward replied.

Having recovered a little, Gordon managed to speak:

"Edward? Who are you talking to?"

"Gordon! I'm pleased that you're okay. I'm speaking to Tommy."

"Who's that?" Gordon asked.

"I'm not sure what he is to you, but you have spoken about him. He knows you. He has called you 'Dad' (whatever that is)."

"Dad . . .?"

Hearing his dad's voice, Tom said, "Yes, it's me, Dad – Tom. I've come to take you home."

"Home . . . what's that? Who are you?" Gordon said, trying hard to make sense of the words.

"What's wrong with him, Edward?"

"It's the effects of that last wave; you have to give him time and, believe me, there's plenty of it here."

"Something is telling me I haven't got a lot of time, Edward. As you said, the longer I'm here the smaller the chance of getting back."

127

Tom assessed the situation. He'd thought that all he had to do was find his father and hold him while the others pulled him back with the rope, but he could see now that plan was ridiculous, especially as he couldn't even locate his father.

"Edward, do you know if there is a way back to the tree?"

"All I know is that it will happen for Gordon when it's gathering time and, as you came in that way, presumably you too."

"How do we know when it's gathering time?" Tom enquired.

"We don't. It just happens."

"What - one minute we're here then there?"

"I forgot, there's a piercing, hissing sound - then it happens; but what I do know is that it's every time there is someone to gather at the place," Edward said.

"Well, at least I have something to work with."

"Have I helped you, Tommy, by telling you that?"

"What was it you told me?" Tom asked.

"I don't know; did I tell you something?"

"Edward, Tom, can you speak to me?" Gordon said, gaining his strength.

"Gordon, it's me – Edward. Your voice doesn't sound so weary; that's good I think, isn't it?"

"Yes, Edward, it is good. I've noticed that the darkness can only focus on one person at a time. I think that's its weakness. While it was doing that I found my memory and strength returning."

"I think it was, as you say, focusing on Tommy and then me."

"Do you know if Tom's okay?"

"Because Tommy has only been here a short while, he is still strong. I think he will be able to speak soon. He asked me something about gathering, or was it the tree?"

"So which was it, Edward - gathering or tree?"

"Why is it so important, Gordon? Surely it doesn't matter here which it was?"

"That's where you're wrong, Edward. If Tom was asking questions about them, I should think they're part of his plan of getting back."

"Back where, Gordon?"

"Home, Edward, home."

"Am I going home too, Gordon?"

"If Tom finds a way – yes, Edward, we'll all be going home."

Chapter Fourteen

"**D**oc, I don't want to alarm you, but there's not many strands left of that rope. I pray he's not in there much longer."

"Yes, I noticed, Pastor. Let me see if I can talk to him. Tom, can you hear me?"

The word 'Tom' was all that could be heard in the speaker before it was lost in a hail of static.

"Tom, you have to get back here now! The rope's breaking and won't last much longer!" Miles shouted into the microphone, hoping Tom could hear him.

"How are his vitals doing, Doc?"

Miles went back to the monitor.

"It appears, Pastor, that the rope isn't the only problem; his vitals are showing hardly any signs of life. *Tom, whatever you plan to do, for heaven's sake, do it now!"* Miles shouted.

"Doc, I'm going to try to see if I can do something to strengthen the rope."

"Like what?"

"Well, there's a long piece of rope that's not doing anything, where it's tied to the tree. I'm thinking if I cut it off and try and join each side to where it's breaking it might buy Tom a bit more time."

"It's worth a try, Pastor."

Having cut the rope, Alec walked towards the tree and was about to tie it, when Miles said, "Pastor, I've just remembered what Tom said. Don't go near the tree, especially now you can see the face. Whatever is in there will take *you*!"

No sooner had he said that, than the pastor felt a force starting to draw him closer to the tree.

"Doc, I need help - something is pulling me!"

"Grab the end of the rope and throw me the other end," Miles shouted.

The pastor quickly obeyed, leaving Miles pulling with all his might.

Once again the place was filled with hissing.

"That hissing sound - is that the *gathering* sound, Edward?" Tom asked.

"You can hear it?" Edward said.

"Yes, can't you?"

"No, and it means that you're being sent to gather. There must be someone near the tree."

"Looks like I'm going with you, Tom; I can hear it as well," Gordon announced.

"Does that mean we will be at the tree at the same time?" Tom asked.

"Yes, Tom. By the way you said that, I take it you have something in mind?" his dad asked.

"The plan was to bring you back; but now, to be honest - I haven't got a clue how, especially as I can't even see where you are. Although, if we are being sent to the tree together, at least we might have a chance to pull this off," Tom said.

"But you know you won't be the only two there; there will be others," Edward said.

"What others?" Tom asked.

"The others that came in that way."

"Are you saying that every time someone is by that tree they are gathered here?" Tom asked, sounding confused.

"Yes, Tommy, they are gathered in from all sorts of places. Everyone is assigned to the place that brought them here - to gather," Edward replied.

"And the people here have no choice?"

"What's 'choice', Tommy?"

"It's free will to . . . choose, I think."

"I don't understand, Tommy; we go without thinking - it's what you do here."

"Well, if it wasn't for the fact that I think it's our way out of here, I'll tell you now, you wouldn't see me obeying whatever it is that rules this place!" Tom shouted out.

"Tom, you shouldn't do that," his dad said.

"Do what?"

"Draw attention to yourself. I was just like you when I came here. The darkness will punish you. It even knows what you are thinking."

"Are you saying that it already knows that I plan to take you out of here?" Tom said.

"Probably, but as no one has ever escaped I don't think you will cause it any concern. And that might be our advantage, Tom," his dad whispered. "Edward, do you remember the arrangement we had to distract its attention from one of us?" he whispered.

"I think so, Gordon. Was it that one of us would draw the attention, so the other one could do something," he whispered back.

"That's it. Listen, when Tom and I are sent to gather, can you do or say something to draw its attention to yourself?"

"I will try, Gordon."

"It sounds as if you're the one with the plan, Dad," Tom said.

"Plan? No, Tom - it's a long shot, but if we can draw its attention away from us at the tree, we might have time to think," his dad replied.

"So, how long before we go?

Before Tom could say another word he felt himself being taken, and found he was looking out through a misty veil at the pastor and Miles.

"Miles! Pastor! Can you hear me?" Tom called.

"At last, Tom! Where are you?" Miles replied, while trying to hang on to the rope.

"I'm here - at the tree. You look as though you're struggling with something."

"You can see us?" Miles asked, excitedly.

"Sort of. It's like looking through frosted glass."

"Pastor Alec's being pulled to the tree!" Miles said, out of breath.

"So it's him who's being gathered! I told you not to go too close to it."

"I know, but we didn't have a choice. We've been trying to tell you the rope is breaking. Pastor was trying to tie another piece to it when he felt a force pulling him. Can you do something your end?" Miles replied.

"The truth is, Miles, I think it's me who's pulling him."

"Don't worry about me, Tom; you get yourself back here!" Pastor Alec called out.

"Tom, are those your friends you're talking to?" his dad asked.

"Dad, you're here?"

"Yes."

"So - can you not see them?"

"No, not until you are finished gathering. It seems that there can only be one person at a time at the portal."

"What's going on? Why the hold up? We are waiting to gather here," demanded an impatient voice, close by.

"Dad, can you somehow home in on my voice?"

"That's easier said than done, Tom; your voice sounds as if it's coming from all directions, but I'll try. Keep talking."

"Tom, I don't want to alarm you, but the rope - it looks as if you only have seconds before it breaks! You have to do whatever you're going to - *now*!" Miles shouted out.

"I'm not ready," Tom replied.

"Tom, if that rope snaps you'll be in there forever!" Miles warned, urgently.

Not wanting to leave his dad, Tom cried out, "Dad, please! You have to be here *now* - it's our only chance!"

"Tom, your voice sounds different - I must be behind you," his dad said.

Tom didn't know if that was enough to get them both out of there when Miles pulled on the rope, but he knew he had no other choice. It was that or be condemned to a life of darkness himself.

"Pull, Miles! Pull!" Tom shouted.

Miles found himself in a dilemma. If he pulled on the rope that was attached to Tom, he would have to let go of the rope that was stopping the pastor from being gathered.

Pastor Alec knew what he was being faced with. Looking into Miles' eyes, he said: "Tell my wife I love her."

And with that, he let go of the rope.

"No!" Miles cried out.

Realising that the pastor was lost, he grabbed the other rope just in time before it snapped, and pulled with all his might.

"Tom, I can't hold it - the force is stronger than me!" he cried out, as his feet were sliding towards the tree.

As Tom's dad was now closer, he could hear the distress in Miles' voice. He knew he had to do something, but *what* he didn't know as he didn't have a body, only a mind.

That's it - the mind! That's why the darkness takes it away. It's our only weapon against it, realised Gordon in a lucid flash.

Instantly a loud hissing surrounded him. Gordon knew it was the darkness – that it had read his thoughts and was now at the portal to stop them. He could feel his mind beginning to go blank.

"Concentrate! I've got to concentrate!" he cried out.

The hissing got louder and louder.

"Ed . . . Edward, I don't know if you can hear me, but I need help to distract the darkness!" he called out.

"My name is Edward. I know how I got here. I can think," came out of the darkness.

For a brief moment, Gordon felt the intensity of the hissing subside. He knew that Edward had managed to distract the darkness.

"Bye, Tom!" he said.

Quickly he mustered up a picture of himself with his arms outstretched, pushing Tom from behind. Tom felt a jolt propelling him forward through the portal.

Miles rushed over, to see his lifeless body lying at the foot of the tree. Quickly he dragged him to a safe distance from it.

"Tom! Tom, speak to me!" he said, trying to find a pulse.

Quickly Miles fetched the defibrillator and waited for it to charge, then attached it to Tom's chest. His lifeless body arched upward. Miles could see that there was a pulse and life had returned.

"Got you!" Miles said, leaning over him.

Tom's eyes flickered, and then opened.

"What happened? Where am I?" he said.

"Don't move, Tom. I need to check you over."

"Who's Tom?" came out of his mouth before he passed out.

Chapter Fifteen

Tom opened his eyes and began to look around.

There was a nurse in the room. She immediately opened the door and went to the nurse's station. "Can you tell Dr Martin his friend is awake?" she said to the person behind the desk.

Miles had just finished talking to one of his patients when he got the message.

"Welcome back, Tom!" Miles said, as he entered room.

Tom was about to say something.

"Don't say anything yet, Tom. I just want to run a few tests on you. Now, without moving your head, let your eyes follow my finger," he said moving his finger from left to right. "I'm going to ask you some questions. Can you tell me your name?"

"I think it must be 'Tom', as you have just called me that."

"Fair enough. Can you remember anything about what happened to you?"

"Happened? What do you mean? What is this place? How did I get here and who are you?"

"It's all right. Nurse, you can go now; I'll let you know when I'm finished here," Miles said, not wanting her to hear anything about what happened to Tom.

Seeing that Tom was suffering from memory loss, he said, "I'm Miles, your friend, and you're in hospital."

"Miles?" Tom said, at a loss as to why he didn't know him.

"Yes, Dr Miles. Can you remember Alec, the pastor? He was your friend too," Miles said to him.

"Pastor? I don't know any pastor. Look, just tell me what's going on. How long have I been here?" Tom said, raising his voice in frustration.

"Two weeks."

"Two weeks! That's insane - I've lost two weeks of my life . . ."

"You don't remember anything at all?"

Tom went quiet, trying to think. "No."

"What about the tree?"

Miles could see that the word 'tree' caused a reaction. "What is it about the tree, Tom?"

"I'm not sure, but there's something in me that's telling me it's important."

"Keep going, Tom - I need you to remember," Miles said.

Tom shut his eyes. "There's a face! I remember a face in the tree and the words: 'Don't touch the tree.' It's my father's voice - coming from the tree."

Tom opened his eyes.

"I remember! I went to the tree to get my father back."

"Can you remember the pastor (and me) with you?"

"You're Miles, the doctor. I remember you, but I can't remember him being there."

"You can't remember the pastor?" Miles asked, surprised.

"All I recall about him was preaching in church."

"So you don't remember having dinner with him and his wife?"

Tom thought for a moment, and then replied, "It's sketchy - I'm not sure. Why is my mind so foggy? What's wrong with me?" Tom said, getting agitated.

"Calm down, Tom. The fogginess will clear. You've been through a lot."

"How can I, when I don't know anything about what I've been through?"

After he calmed down, he said, "By the way, where is he? Aren't pastors supposed to visit people who are in hospital?"

"Even if he wanted to, Tom, he can't."

"I suppose he's busy out there, saving souls? Some friend he turned out to be."

"I don't think you know, Tom, how much of a friend he was to you," Miles replied.

"Was?" Tom said. "So, isn't he my friend now? Did we have a falling out or something?"

"Of course you didn't - far from it. I mean: he's gone," Miles said, sadly.

"Gone where?" Tom asked.

Miles knew he had to tell him, but he also knew that now wasn't the right time.

"Tom, I think you ought to get some rest. Your mind needs time to process what's been said here today. I'll come and see you tomorrow."

"You're not going to tell me where the pastor's gone?" Tom asked Miles as he made his way to the door.

"I'll tell you tomorrow, Tom. Now get some rest," Miles replied.

Miles walked into the room, to see Tom sitting on the bed dressing.

"What do you think you're doing, Tom?" he said.

"Getting out of here. I'm going home."

"Where's home, Tom?" Miles said, to see if his memory had come back completely.

"It's . . ."

"Tom, you're not ready to leave yet. Look, stay another day."

"I need to get out of here, Miles. I can't lay here any longer, not knowing what's happened. I need to find answers and I'm not finding them here."

"How are you going to find answers, when you don't even know where you live?"

"Well, if you were to take me home, I know my memory would come back sooner than being here."

Miles knew Tom had a point as he knew familiar surroundings can help people who have memory loss.

"So what do you reckon? Can you remember this place?" Miles asked, as they came through the door.

"Give me time to settle in and I will do," Tom replied, going from room to room.

He opened the door to his office and noticed a large collection of books on the shelf. They all had similar titles: nearly every one of them was about 'Pareidolia'. He took one off the shelf and sat behind his desk. He was about to open it, when Miles asked: "Have you got any coffee here? I could do with a cup."

"Yes, left-hand top cupboard above the sink."

Miles smiled to himself. He knew that, although Tom's memory was a bit sketchy, he was going to be okay.

Tom browsed through the book and noticed that there were many underlined sentences and references, which he started to read. But, then his attention was drawn to the file of notes written by him, on the side of his desk. The top sheet revealed details and a list of things he needed to assist him in getting his father back.

"Back from where?" he thought to himself.

"Are your papers helping?" Miles said, coming in with the coffees.

"I've just seen a list I made. It says that I need them to get my father back. Back from where, Miles? Do you know?"

"Don't you remember, Tom? Back at the hospital you remembered the tree, and you said you heard your father's voice?"

"Did I?"

"Yes, Tom."

"Look, Miles, I know you want me to remember what happened on my own, but I think it's going to be easier if you tell me everything."

"Okay, Tom. Yes, I was hoping it would come back without me telling you. Your father was taken by the Pareidolia. He's trapped in their world, and so you set out (along with the pastor and me) to bring him home."

"Hence all the books I've got on the subject," Tom said.

"I suppose so. I didn't realise you had so many."

Miles went on to tell him what had happened.

"So I failed to bring him home," Tom said, sadly.

"Tom, you were facing the unknown. The pastor would say that the fact that you went there, and got back, was a miracle."

"Yes - the pastor. You say he went with us. Why do I have a feeling you're keeping something from me - about him?" Tom asked.

"The Pareidiola have him."

"How did that happen?"

"I was left with the impossible choice of saving either you or him. He made the choice for me, Tom. He sacrificed himself so that you could live."

Tom didn't say anything; he just sat there. The words of Alice came back to him. "I know if he had to give his life for a friend he wouldn't hesitate."

"Tom, are you okay? This is the reason I haven't told you. I was hoping you would remember it yourself."

"I can't take it in. I know she said that, but you never think it's actually going to happen. I take it you've spoken to Alice?"

"Yes, surprisingly she took it well; she seemed to have so much peace about her."

"Peace! Considering her husband has disappeared into another world, I don't know how she can have peace."

"You forget, Tom, she is a devoted woman of God, which is where peace that passes all understanding comes from."

Miles looked at his watch. "Look, I've got a meeting at five; I'm going to have to leave you. I'm writing my number down on your pad. Ring me if you need me. I'll ring you tonight to make sure you're okay."

"Yes, that's fine. I'll be all right; I've heard enough to keep me occupied."

Tom went back to reading his notes, hoping to remember more. The evening passed and, as he was feeling tired, he knew it was time for him to get to bed. The first thing he noticed when he went into the room was a white stone on his bedside table. As he got closer, he saw what seemed to be a face on it. He knew that, for it to be there, it must be in connection with his study on Pareidolia. He sat on the bed and picked it up.

"Hello, Tommy. It's nice to see you. I've had doubts about whether I would see you again. Your father asked me if I'd seen you; he was concerned that maybe the effects of passing back through the portal may have killed you," Edward said.

When he heard a voice coming from the stone, Tom dropped it. He couldn't believe it was speaking to him.

"Tommy, it's me Edward; don't you know me?"

"How's this possible? Am I really hearing a stone talking to me?"

"Yes, Tommy, we've always talked to each other. Your father will be so pleased that I've spoken to you, and the pastor will."

Tom picked it up; the minute he did an electric charge went through him and knocked him back on the bed. Sitting back up, he said, "Edward! You're Edward - I remember now."

"Yes, your father gave me that name."

"Father! Yes, he's there with you. I tried to get him back."

"That was the plan you had when you were here. Your father realised you were having problems. He knew he wasn't going to make it back with you, so he helped you through the portal."

"Edward, you mentioned the pastor. Is he there with you?"

"Oh yes, Tommy. He's here all right. I thought your father coming here caused chaos, but the pastor - he's non-stop. What he says is *preaching*. For the first time here, there's light."

"Light?" Tom exclaimed.

"Yes, it's coming from him. The more he preaches, the brighter the light."

"I bet the darkness doesn't like that," Tom replied.

"No. It doesn't matter what it tries to do, it can't stop the pastor. People are communicating with each other, and disappearing from here after the pastor has preached. It's a different place, Tommy. Now there's hope."

"Edward, can I give you a message for the pastor?"

"Of course you can."

"Tell him thank you for what he did, and tell my father that I love him," Tom said.

"This word 'love': I have heard the pastor use it. I take it it's a good word?"

"Yes, Edward it is; it's a very good word. You know, now that I've remembered everything, I have to write it down - so I don't ever forget. I'm going back into my study to do it."

Tom immediately went to his desk, put down the stone and began to write.

'My name's Professor Tom Harvey, and what I'm about to tell you I will have to say quickly in case the memory of it is taken from me. It will take you beyond the realm of your wildest imagination. What would you say if I told you that there is a world, separated by a thin vale, that runs parallel to this world, far from anything that we know here? Where its occupants know nothing but darkness, despair and torment? Where their sole purpose is to gather beings from this world into theirs? The day they gathered my father was the start of a life-changing event that sent me on a quest to try and get him back. I found out that, once there, there would be no way back, but I had to try. This is my story. Is it true? Am I insane? That will be for you to judge when I've finished telling you. My name is Professor Tom Harvey and

I have come to warn you of the World of Pareidolia.'

"Now I can relax, Edward. So, you say there's World War Three going on there?"

"What's 'World War Three'?" Edward asked.

"Sorry, Edward. How can I put it simply?"

Tom thought for a moment, and then said, "The balance there has been upset big-time?"

"Balance, yes - I see what you mean. It *has* been World War Three since the pastor has been here. I think the darkness might be losi . . . Ah, ah!" Edward cried out, unable to finish.

"Edward! Are you all right? Speak to me!"

There was silence for a minute, and then it was broken by the words: "Tom, I'm all right. Can you pick me up?"

"Sure."

The next thing Tom realised was that he was back in the world of the Pareidolia.

"Edward! Why did you gather me?" Tom cried out.

"He didn't, Tom. The darkness did."

"Dad, is that you?"

"Yes, Tom."

"I don't understand what happened," Tom replied.

"The darkness knew it was powerless to stop the pastor, and took it out on Edward. It was so powerful that we all felt it when it was directed at him. I don't think Edward's coming back from that," his father said.

"I should have known there was something wrong! The voice sounded like Edward's, but he called me 'Tom' and Edward always called me 'Tommy'. So, it looks like it's just the three of us taking on the evil in this place."

"Hi Tom, it's me - the pastor. I'd like to say it's nice to speak to you again, but I never thought it would be in such a place. *Now* you know why I harked on about life insurance. I am so pleased you accepted it, because now you are safe from the evil here."

"Yes - about that: then why am I here? And, more importantly, (you being a pastor): how come you're here?"

"Tom, it's obvious - can't you see? The Lord is using us and, when our work is done here, He will take us out."

"And Dad?" Tom asked.

"Don't worry, Tom, I've accepted the pastor's 'insurance'."

"Tom! Are you in there?" Miles shouted through the letterbox of Tom's apartment.

As he hadn't been able to contact him on the phone, he'd called round - in case Tom had become unwell.

"Can I help you?" said a voice behind him, as he was bending down trying to look through the letterbox.

Miles stood up and turned around. "Yes, I've come to check on my friend, Tom."

"He's at work. He's never here on Wednesdays. It's the day I clean the place."

"Then you have a key to get in?" Miles asked her.

"Of course I do; how else am I to get in?" the cleaner said.

"Look, I'm his doctor. I brought him home last night - he hasn't been well. I need to get in to make sure he's okay. He hasn't been answering his phone, and now I can't get answer from inside. Can you open the door please?"

The cleaner quickly opened the door, letting Miles go in ahead of her.

"Tom! Tom!" Miles called out, going from room to room.

Checking the bedroom, he could see that the bed hadn't been slept in. Having checked every room bar the study, Miles made his way there.

He rushed into the room to see that it was empty. Open on the desk was Tom's notebook.

Miles could see yesterday's date at the top of the page and that Tom had written several lines, but it didn't give any clues has to where he was.

"Tom, where are you?" he said aloud.

Perplexed, he sat down in Tom's chair and scratched his chin. As he did so, his eyes went to the white stone on the desk. Miles reached over to pick it up, when an alarming voice came from the stone:

"*Miles - don't touch it!*"

But it was too late.

Authors note

More books by Paul Fronda

SBN 9780993013249

What forces of good and evil were at work that made their presence felt and seen to eight total strangers? Each one, at their lowest ebb in life and looking for a way out of their circumstances, found they were alone in the woods, not knowing what would befall them in that dark place.

Which force would they listen too? One would save them, taking them to a place of safety, the other to a dark place of no return. The choice was theirs.

What they experienced was so strange that they didn't know what was real. They were eight normal, rational people, but now they found themselves believing the impossible, which led them on a mission to find the answer to the question: Why us?

As you read their stories you might be thinking that such things could never happen to you. But consider: what if you woke tomorrow and found that your life had completely changed? What if you found yourself wandering along a track in that dark wood, not knowing your fate? How would you react if you were to become one of those who would experience that life-changing event, which was so far out of the realms of normality?

Who would believe your story?

ISBN 978-09930132-6-3

Some people say a curse can only harm you if you believe in it, and Cathy Derwin was one of those who didn't believe. But the evil curse spoken by Tobias Spry, as he was being burnt to death all those centuries ago, was so strong that her disbelief would be futile against its evil power. One by one her ancestors had succumbed to the curse as it pursued them through the centuries, and now it was her time to face the evil curse of Tobias Spry.

From the snares
of the Devil,
deliver us, O Lord.

BALOR'S REVENGE

Paul Fronda

ISBN978-0-9930132-9-4

A young American couple are intrigued to hear about a mysterious inheritance left to them in Ireland. They travel to the Emerald Isle to satisfy their curiosity, but they discover a lot more they bargained for. They find the country and the people charming, but they are unsettled by strange events and chilling, dark warnings.

Should they ignore the dire predictions of the roadside tinker,
or dismiss them as old blarney?

Had they known what evil was about to unfold, they would have never
put their feet on Irish soil.

Made in the USA
Lexington, KY
16 March 2017